DATE			

10-07

What if?...

Inside, not all is what it seems.
Inside these covers, five women face the
deterministic trap of fate... and what they find
may surprise you.

In this intriguing mosaic novel connected by a mysterious, obscuring mist, five women of different ages face off with fate. A freshman at a girls' boarding school bears the strange ability to share others' dreams. For a young woman in a straitjacket, it's her desperate task to pick a very particular future from among countless possibilities; for a middle-aged skier, it's refusing to be a puppet on a string. For a veteran fortune teller, it's a suddenly faltering faith in her own trade. And for an elderly lady whose precious alarm clock stops operating, it's a vivid and troubling encounter with her own past.

From World Fantasy Award winner Zoran Živković comes *Steps Through the Mist*, another masterpiece of the mind.

Step this way through the mist...

Accolades

Praise for *Seven Touches of Music*

"And then, every so often, you come across a work whose vividness and vitality are so abundant they seem to transcend language. The Serbian author Zoran Živković... already has many passionate supporters in America, and though it is too soon to crown him the new Borges, *Seven Touches of Music* makes him a leading candidate for the position."

New York Times Book Review

"The stories are simple vignettes but they hit with a punch that leaves you thinking... Translated from the Serbian by Alice Copple-Tošić, the stories read smoothly and with a lyricism to the language that is itself almost musical."

SFRevu

"Think of Borges and Calvino, or Jeff Vandermeer. Then erase your brain, or really, no need. Živković will do that for you. He has that gift of effortless prose that envelops you and is startlingly easy to read even as it drives daggers into your perception of the world as well as your heart."

Rick Kleffel, The Agony Column

"Written in Živković's trademark style and bringing to life the crisp, obscure magic that is typical of his work... *Seven Touches of Music* is a showpiece."

HorrorScope (Australia)

"While physics continues its search for a unifying theory, Živković works at unifying literature, showing the value of creativity and speculative imagination in understanding our world and universe."

Fantasy Book Spot

"Mr. Živković's stories are gems... This is a book to savor, to read and reread, to love."

Ideomancer

"This velvety hardcover edition perfectly suits Zoran Živković's elegant writing style, for which we should also give some credit to translator Alice Copple-Tošić. Živković's prose is spare and understated, yet he can make the simplest story elements bear a heavy emotional weight... The stories are all superbly crafted and emotionally charged."

Fantastic Reviews

"The stories range in emotion from humor to poignancy to chilling. [Filled] with highly nuanced *what ifs* that use their musical themes to construct a literary ensemble of thoughtful pieces... Reading this work is like sipping from a wine glass and swirling it around to get its true taste."

Heartland Reviews

Steps Through the Mist

a mosaic novel

Zoran Živković

translated from the Serbian
by Alice Copple-Tošić

aio
Aio Publishing Company, LLC

Published by Aio Publishing Company, LLC
Charleston, South Carolina, USA

This book is printed on acid-free, recycled paper.

All characters and events in this book are fictitious. Any resemblance to
persons living or dead is strictly coincidental.

LIBRARY OF CONGRESS CATALOGING-IN-PUBLICATION DATA
Živković, Zoran.
  [Koraci kroz maglu. English]
  Steps through the mist : a mosaic novel / Zoran Živković
    p. cm.
  ISBN 978-1-933083-10-0 (alk. paper)
  1. Zoran Živković--Translations into English. I. Title.

  PG1419.36.I95413K67 2007
  891.8'236--dc22

        2007017559

Printed and bound in the United States of America.

To Tamar Yellin, a great writer

Steps Through the Mist

Contents

disorder in the head

1

Miss Emily opened the door to the first-year classroom at the girls' boarding school. The quiet murmuring of twenty-six freshmen subsided and they all stood up as though by command. They were wearing identical navy blue dresses that reached down to the mid-calf and buttoned up to the chin, completely plain, without the least embellishment. Even the buttons were covered with the same blue cloth. Only the white collars of their blouses interrupted this uniformity, varying slightly in shape. Not a single girl wore her hair loose; they all wore braids.

Miss Emily's brown dress was of the same plain cut as her students' uniforms. There was a small brooch pinned to its left-hand side that almost blended into the background. Her dark hair, streaked with gray despite its lingering thickness, was pulled back into a bun. Her tiny eyes gazed mouse-like through her round wire-framed glasses. The low heels of her high-topped shoes did not add much to Miss Emily's height. She was still shorter than most of the sixteen-year-old girls who were now waiting, motionlessly, for the signal to sit down.

She went up to the desk and set down a stack of papers and a leather glasses case. Her eyes passed over her students and she nodded briefly. The room was filled with the rustling of dresses and scraping of chairs, and then she too sat down. She set her spine firmly against the back of the chair, from which it would not move until the end of the class, as though glued in place. Only her head in lively movement would be at variance with this stiff body.

First, she concentrated on arranging the objects in front of her. In addition to those she had brought, there was a small vase containing two purple wildflowers, a wooden pen holder, a long thin pointer, a large globe and a glass half-filled with water, covered by a linen napkin. She did not strive for any special pattern. The priority was that everything be lined up, to offset any impression of randomness. She abhorred disorder, both external and internal.

"Good morning, young ladies." Her feeble voice matched her stature.

"Good morning, Miss Emily," chimed twenty-six voices all together.

"I hope you slept well. From what you have written I can see that some of you are not getting the rest you need at night, particularly at your age."

She stopped talking and laid her hands on the pile of papers in front of her. It was a collection of dreams. Whenever she commenced teaching a new class, the first thing she did was have the freshmen write down their dreams of the previous night. This was the best way to get to know them. Nothing spoke more eloquently about the girls than what they dreamed. It was here that they showed their true nature. In addition, dreams are the first indication of the disorder that threatens to overwhelm young minds. And that could only be thwarted if discovered in time, before it seriously corrupted the personality. After that it was very difficult, perhaps even impossible, to remove.

Of course, there were always freshmen who would try to deceive her. They wrote unauthentic accounts of their dreams, resorting to invention for various reasons. Some simply had not dreamed anything or could not remember their dreams, but were reluctant to admit this. Others were ashamed of their dreams. The most dangerous, however, were those who made them up in order to outsmart her. Those were the girls in need of special attention. Such duplicity was a clear sign of a wayward disposition. What she found additionally offensive was the fact that they underestimated her. As though it were that easy to deceive her! With experience measured in decades, she was able to recognize without fail not only false dreams but those calculated to poke fun at her.

Among the twenty-six papers that had been given to her

at the end of the last class, she was certain that three belonged to this latter type. They were all signed, but since she still didn't know the girls, their names meant nothing to her. All the same, she would soon see which of the young ladies considered themselves smarter than she. Nothing would teach them a better lesson than to experience a little public humiliation. They had to find out immediately that they would reap what they sowed. There could be no leniency in this regard. It was the only way to set them on the right path.

She took the first sheet from the pile and turned it over. At the bottom, next to the girl's signature, Miss Emily had written a great warning sign in red ink: three horizontal parallel lines cut by a vertical line. She used many similar symbols, with meanings known only to herself. Generations of freshmen had done their utmost to break these codes, but none had succeeded as yet. To make them even harder to decipher, Miss Emily periodically introduced confusing changes that made sense only to her: new signs appeared and old ones changed their meaning.

"Will Miss Alexandra please stand up."

At the penultimate desk of the row next to the window a willowy girl with large eyes and prominent cheekbones rose to her feet. Miss Emily examined her carefully. Not at all unexpected. These freshmen who got their height early were the first to have swollen egos. They thought they were special because they were taller than their classmates and more attractive. As if that could make them superior! But she had a remedy for such overconfidence.

"Ah, that's who you are. Fine." She put Miss Alexandra's paper to one side and then took another one from the pile. "Now would Miss Theodora please be so kind as to introduce herself."

A plump girl in the third desk of the middle row slowly stood up. She had red hair with curls that not even the tight braids could straighten completely. Her face was sprinkled with freckles. Miss Emily pulled up the collar of her dress slightly around her neck. She didn't like freckles at all. They were a mark. There was always a reason for them, as was evident this very instant. It was, of course, no accident that she had singled out this girl's dream.

"There you are. Very good." Miss Emily held up a third paper with a warning sign on it. "The last one to introduce herself is Miss Clara."

A short girl wearing thick glasses stood up in the first row, in the desk by the door. Her head was bowed and her right hand was clutching the three middle fingers of her left hand. Strange, thought Miss Emily. Of all the freshmen this is the last one I would have suspected. She could almost recognize herself some forty years ago. But experience had taught her how deceptive appearances can be. Even though Miss Clara seemed the epitome of modesty, what she had written clearly indicated that was merely a superficial impression.

"All right. Now would the rest of you girls take a good look at the three who are standing."

This caused a stir. The girls who were sitting started to look around in bewilderment, staring at the three standing girls, who were just as confused. Several neighboring heads drew together and whispered. Miss Emily let the uncertainty gain momentum. She had put on this show many times and knew exactly when to speak again.

"You don't see anything unusual?" she asked at last. All the faces turned toward her. "I don't blame you. There's nothing that can be seen. One would say there is nothing special about Alexandra, Theodora and Clara. But this is not so. There are things that cannot be discerned by the eye because they are hidden. Terrible things that are not the least fitting in the honorable individuals that we all hope you will become after you leave this school. One such thing is a penchant for lying."

Miss Emily paused to allow her words full impact.

"This is a very bad characteristic. It is particularly dangerous when it appears in younger individuals. A girl who starts to lie early in life will most certainly not stop there. What inevitably awaits her is a wayward life of even worse sins. All lies, however, are not the same. Although no lie can be justified, some can be understood to a certain extent. Let's take, for example, your compositions on what you dreamed. Almost half are not true. You thought you could fool me, but that, of course, is impossible. I am quite capable of telling real dreams from false. I do not hold it very much against most of you, though, this resort to fabrication. You did not act out of ulterior motives. You found yourselves in an awkward position and lying seemed the only way out of it. You will learn in time that sincerity always serves you best in any difficulty you might encounter."

Miss Emily took the pointer and started to draw it back and forth through the closed fist of her left hand.

"But the motives of these three young ladies were not in the least naive. Their fabrications were fully intentional. They treated me condescendingly, wanting to show their superiority. Arrogance went along with the lies, and it is hard to find a worse combination. They were convinced I would not see through them, but they have greatly underestimated me. Now the time has come to face the consequences. It is always unpleasant, but cannot be escaped. In any case, it is for their own good. Confession and repentance are the first steps toward redemption and healing."

The pointer stopped moving. A hush filled the room for several moments.

"So? Let's hear what you have to say."

It was not clear which of the girls was expected to speak first. Miss Alexandra glanced questioningly at Miss Theodora, who replied with a shrug of the shoulders. Miss Clara kept her head bowed. Her eyes had become glassy and wet. The tears had not yet started to flow, but it was certain that nothing could stop them. The tension in the classroom grew along with the look of impatience on Miss Emily's face.

"They didn't lie."

The voice was soft and came from somewhere in the back. A multitude of braids swung when the inquisitive heads quickly turned around to look. Miss Emily twisted her neck.

"Who said that?"

The girl who rose from behind the last desk in the middle row did not stand out in any way. She was thin, with dark hair and regular features, quite common among the uniformed girls. Only her eyes set her apart. Miss Emily knew about such eyes— and didn't like them. Behind their clarity, vivacity and penetrating power stood a character that was most difficult to handle. Willful and persistent, it resisted submission and molding, and served as a very bad example to the other girls. She had to be cautious from the very start.

"What is your name?"

"Miss Irena."

The name sounded familiar to Miss Emily. She had taken note of it while reading the girls' dream compositions, but forgot why. She took the pile of papers from the desk and started to leaf through it. She had gone through about one third of them when she suddenly remembered. The paper she was looking for was at the very bottom. She had left it there, intending to address that case at the end, after finishing with the ordinary ones. It was quite unusual. Over the years she had received a wide variety of compositions, but it had never happened that a girl would turn in a paper with only a signature and nothing else.

"Ah, you are the one. Very nice. And this was your dream?"

Miss Emily raised the empty sheet of paper so all the girls could have a good look.

"Yes."

"Should we conclude, based on this, that you didn't dream anything?"

"No, you shouldn't."

"So that's it. You did have a dream, but for some reason you did not consider it necessary to inform us about it. Would you perhaps tell us the reason?"

"I did tell you the dream."

"You told us? I don't see any report here. Do any of you freshmen see better than I do?"

She began turning the page over slowly from one side to the other, making an arc with it in front of her. The question was not directed at anyone in particular, but several girls nonetheless briefly shook their heads.

"It's mist."

Miss Emily's mouse-like eyes immediately squinted.

"I don't think I heard you too well."

"That's mist," repeated the girl from the end of the middle row. "I always dream about mist."

"You dream about mist?"

"Yes."

Miss Emily put the pointer down, then adjusted its position a little so it was parallel to the edge of the desk.

"Very interesting. You only dream about mist? You must be very bored when you sleep."

"I'm not. There's another dream."

"Oh, there is? So why didn't you write about that other one?"

"Because it isn't mine."

"It isn't yours? Then whose is it?"

"Someone else's."

"How can something in your dream belong to someone else?"

"It's no longer my dream. The mist suddenly disperses and I enter someone else's dream. I dream what others dream."

Miss Emily looked at Miss Irena for several moments without speaking.

"My dear, I have heard all manner of concoctions from freshmen during my many years of tenure at this school, but I must admit that you have outdone them all. Do you really expect us to believe what you just said?"

"Yes." The girl's voice was even, as though confirming something quite ordinary.

"And just why should we believe you, might I ask?"

"Because it is the truth."

"How can the truth be that you dream other people's dreams? Has anyone else ever heard of something like that?"

Her eyes swept over the class, but this time not a single head moved. Miss Emily felt awkward. The conversation had taken an unexpected turn and she was no longer in complete control. She had to put an end to this nonsense as soon as possible.

"I think that's enough for now," she continued. "I must warn you that you won't get very far with such stories. A rich imagination is not greatly appreciated here. Other virtues are fostered in this school."

"It's not my imagination. If it were, how would I know that these other girls aren't lying?"

"Of course they lied. I should think I'm the best one to know that. And you are no better than they are. You have not only concocted rubbish, but stubbornly insist it is true."

"I can tell you their dreams. I dreamed them along with them."

Miss Emily's first thought was to resort to her tested procedure. Miss Irena should leave the class at once and report to the principal. Such impudence had to be properly punished. As a lesson to the others. But if she did that, she would be admitting defeat. She had been offered a challenge and had to reply. In any case, why not? Let the girl say what she had to say. She would only embarrass herself. Of course she could not know what the three girls had dreamed. Particularly since these weren't their real dreams, but fabrications.

"All right then. Let's hear. It will give us a fine chance to see that lies are always short-lived."

"Miss Alexandra dreamed that she was in an asylum for the mentally disturbed after a traffic accident in which she hurt her head. She had terrible visions that frightened her. A doctor came to visit and she told him about her visions, but he didn't believe them. Miss Theodora dreamed that she was skiing. An unusually dressed man sat next to her on the ski lift. He explained that he was not there by accident. He had come to see which path she would take to ski down the slope. For some reason this was very important. Miss Clara dreamed that she was a clairvoyant. A young man came to her parlor with a strange request. He wanted her to confirm that he only had a short time left to live."

When Miss Irena finished, the girls kept their heads turned in her direction several moments longer, then all turned toward Miss Emily. Only Miss Alexandra and Miss Theodora continued to stare at the last desk in the middle row. All that broke the silence was the sniffles and sobs of Miss Clara, who had not moved since she first stood up.

Miss Emily's face flushed with anger. There had always been girls who considered themselves smarter than she, at least in the beginning, but something like this had never happened before. This was a true conspiracy! Four of the freshmen had plotted to make her look foolish. Fine! Now they would find out just what they were up against.

"Did you really think this would work? That I am gullible enough to fall for your ploy? That I would believe this nonsense about dreaming other people's dreams, when there is a far simpler and more natural explanation? You found out that I always assign a composition about dreams at the first class. That is no secret, in any case. Then you cleverly planned this whole thing. Three would write invented dreams and one would ostensibly know about them. Your plan, unfortunately, didn't succeed. If you wanted to outsmart me you should have devised something much more convincing. Now you will all go—"

"I was in your dream, too."

Miss Emily quite disliked being interrupted in the middle of a sentence. In any other situation she would have severely reprimanded a freshman impertinent enough to do such a thing. This time, however, there was no reprimand. Staring into the clear eyes at the other end of the classroom, irritated above all by their composure, she picked up the pointer again. She held onto the middle of it tightly with both hands.

"Really? You did me the honor of visiting my dream too? And just what was that dream, if you please?"

"The one you dream all the time. Night after night. The dream about the old woman whose alarm clock is broken and she goes to the watchmaker's... "

The crack of the dry wood breaking in Miss Emily's hands echoed so loudly that several of the girls flinched. Miss Clara raised her tear-streaked face in fear.

"Enough! We don't want to hear your drivel anymore. Leave at once and report to the principal. You others sit down. I'll take care of you later."

The three girls quickly took their seats, but Miss Irena did not head for the door.

"It wouldn't be a good idea for me to go."

This was insubordination. Miss Emily had given an order and it had to be carried out without question. But suddenly her destabilized authority did not seem so important.

"It wouldn't? You don't think, by any chance, that we will miss your company?"

"You will. In a way. If I leave the classroom, it will cease to exist."

Miss Emily stood up slowly. She had never done this before in the middle of a class. Without the chair back, she felt somehow without support, as though floating. She put the two parts of the broken pointer on the desk, briefly bemoaning their mismatched appearance, their slightly different lengths.

"We had no idea that someone so important was with us."

"I'm not at all important. Quite the contrary. I am very secondary. This is not my dream. I am only a guest in it, as usual. But when I leave it, the dream will cease to be. All of this will disappear. There is nothing on the other side of the door but mist. Do you still want me to go and report to the principal?"

The classroom sank into silence. Miss Emily could almost feel the girls' eyes on her: confused, questioning, expectant, frightened. Had she been alone with Miss Irena, she might have given another answer. This way, she had no choice.

"Yes. That is a risk that we must take."

Miss Irena walked along the aisle with slow steps. She

reached the door and put her hand on the knob. She stayed like that for several moments, as though pondering whether or not to say anything, but she didn't utter a word. She turned the knob and the door started to open.

Miss Emily did not see what was on the other side. She quickly turned her head the other way and stared out of the tall windows at the sunny summer morning. She kept her eyes turned in that direction as the door slowly closed behind the girl.

hole in the wall

2

The hospital attendant walking in front of me went up to door number seven on the left. It was made of white metal, like all the others in the hall. Against the dark red wall they looked like widely spaced teeth in a giant jaw. He unbolted a small rectangular peephole, opened it, peered inside briefly, then bolted it again.

"You shouldn't have any trouble with her. We put her in a straitjacket, but not because she's aggressive toward others. She tried to commit suicide, as you know." He indicated the file I was holding. "Just in case, I'll stay close by. If you need me, all you have to do is call."

I nodded. The attendant took a magnetic card out of the breast pocket on his white coat, swiped it through the small terminal by the doorframe and opened the door. He let me go in, but didn't close the door after me. He stayed there, watching. I turned toward him and nodded once again. The heavy door closed on its hinges almost soundlessly and the attendant's large figure disappeared behind it.

I have never liked the white color of the padding that lines the walls and floors of these rooms, as though someone has taken great pains to increase the anxiety of the patients forced to spend time there. The same can be said of the bright fluorescent lighting that is never turned off, nor even turned down during the night. The only thing that disrupted the depressive uniformity of the room was a small window high up next to the ceiling on the wall facing the door. It was actually a ventilation shaft with two thick vertical bars instead of glass. This metal protection was quite superfluous; it was impossible to climb up there even if a person were unencumbered by a straitjacket, and nothing larger than a cat could squeeze through it.

The girl was sitting under that opening, her back leaning against the wall. Her legs were bent and her chin was resting on her knees. She looked at me, smiling. I recognized the person whose photo I'd seen in the hospital file: a round face, large, lively brown eyes, small ears, a short, slightly turned-up nose. Dark blond hair reached to her shoulders. Only a rough attempt had been made to comb it, but this did little to diminish the discreet beauty of her face. As it was, her uncombed hair actually made her look younger; if I hadn't known that she was twenty-six, I wouldn't have given her more than twenty-two or twenty-three years.

I dropped to the floor myself, leaning against the door. I always try to put myself at the same level as my patients. As a rule, this creates an impression of equality and helps establish contact with them. I stretched out both legs so the bottoms of my shoes touched the easily soiled padding as little as possible. I put the green file on the floor next to me.

"Hello, Miss Katarina," I said, returning her smile. "How are you?"

"Hello, doctor. I'm fine now. I'm glad you came."

"Let me introduce myself. I'm Dr. Alexander. I'm replacing Dr. Sonja who has been in charge of you up to now. She had an accident and will be absent from work for two or three weeks. Luckily it wasn't anything serious. She fell down the stairs in her house and shattered her shin. Her leg is in a cast, but she's in fine spirits. She's slowly getting used to the crutches."

"Poor Dr. Sonja. Please tell her that I'm terribly sorry about what happened. It must have been quite painful. But, as you say, she'll get well soon. There won't be any consequences. She'll forget both the pain and the crutches."

"I hope so."

"Believe me, that's what will happen."

We looked at each other for a few moments without talking. Finally, I tapped the file on the floor. "Yes, you would know that, wouldn't you? If I've understood correctly, you feel you are able to see the future?"

"I am," she replied in an even voice, as though saying something quite banal.

"Perhaps you could have warned Dr. Sonja of the trouble that awaited her." I said this cheerfully, in jest, certainly with no sound of reproach.

"Perhaps. But even if I had, it would have made no difference. Dr. Sonja didn't believe me."

"It's not easy to believe something like that."

"I know. That's why it's easy to put someone in a place like this just because they claim they can see the future, even if it poses no threat to anyone." There was no reproach in her voice either.

"You are a threat to your own self. That is primarily why people end up here, not because they feel they possess unusual abilities. Didn't you stop eating? And then try to commit suicide?"

"It was a clumsy, slapdash attempt. Mistaken, in any case."

Silence reigned once more. I glanced at my outstretched legs and then looked at her again. She was still smiling.

"There's something I don't understand," I said, shaking my head. "It's odd that your file makes no mention of it. I don't know why Dr. Sonja neglected to talk to you about something that seems to me pivotal to the whole matter: what it was that led you to attempt suicide. If what you claim is true, that you have the gift of seeing the future, then you are the last person in the world one would expect to kill herself. Many people would give their eye teeth to be in your place. It's hard even to imagine all the possibilities available to someone who knows what the future will bring."

"Of course Dr. Sonja wanted to know why I tried to kill myself. But I refused to talk about it."

"Why?"

"There was a reason."

"There was? Does it still exist?"

She didn't reply at once. A questioning look flickered across her face, conveying some hesitation.

"How do you picture the future?" She answered at last with a question.

She'd caught me off guard. I scratched the top of my head as I do automatically when something puzzles me, then I shrugged my shoulders.

"I don't know. I haven't thought about it very much. As a time that is to come, I suppose?" Even as I spoke I realized this was highly unoriginal. I feared I'd earned her derision, but there was none forthcoming.

"Until recently, that was the same attitude I had toward the future," she said in a voice full of understanding. "What will be will be. A person has little influence, if any at all. We enter the mist, not knowing what awaits us there. Then, after the accident, everything changed."

She motioned her head toward the file. This released her from the obligation of having to explain. She had rightly assumed that I'd studied her file thoroughly before coming to see her. She'd been in a serious traffic accident some three and a half months before. She was the only one of four passengers to survive. And just barely. At first the doctors gave her little chance. Although there hadn't been much bodily injury, she had hit her head, resulting in a deep coma. It had taken seventy-three days for her to come out of it. At first there seemed to be no harmful consequences, but soon afterward she started claiming she could see the future. Of course, no one took her seriously. Similar notions appear sometimes among those who have had severe head injuries. Faced with this skepticism, Katarina first withdrew in protest, almost autistically, and then refused to eat. The surgeons soon realized she was no longer within their domain, so they sent her straight from the hospital to us.

Naturally, not a bit of real progress could be expected in the mere two weeks that Dr. Sonja had been working with her. As a rule, such patients require considerable time and patience. It was enough that the doctor had gotten her to eat again. This good sign, however, was soon darkened by the unexpected suicide attempt four days previously. Fortunately, as Katarina said herself, it had been a rather clumsy attempt, easily thwarted. The rules had then required that she be transferred to this room for a while as a precautionary measure

"In what sense did things change?" I asked.

Katarina stretched out her legs like mine and shook her head a bit to loosen her hair. These were the only two parts of her body that she could freely move. The bottoms of her pajamas rose a bit above her socks, revealing part of her calves. I knew quite well how uncomfortable she must have been with her arms confined in the straitjacket, but I could not change that as yet.

"The mist lifted," she replied tersely.

I waited to see if she would say anything more, but when nothing was forthcoming I spoke again.

"And the future was revealed to you?" I tried to say this without the slightest skepticism, as though stating an obvious fact.

She shook her head. "There isn't just one future. That's what confused me the most at first."

"What do you mean?"

She hesitated briefly. "It's a beam... enormous... As soon as I close my eyes, in a waking state, it's there. I see it clearly, it fills my whole field of vision under my closed eyelids. There's nothing else but the beam. It consists of an infinite number of thin strands that seem to be made of frosted glass. Each of them is a future."

She stopped a moment, as though wanting to let me absorb this image.

"But they cannot all become... real. What I mean to say... " I thought I knew what I wanted to say, but somehow I couldn't find the right words. I don't have much experience in talking about the future.

"They can't, that's it. Only one will be real in the end. But until this happens, they are all equally possible. Each of these strands. Completely equal. Until one singles itself out."

"Singles itself out?" I repeated.

"Yes. It starts to shine with an internal glow, turning transparent and expanding at the same time, pushing the others into the background. In the end it fills up the beam's whole space. That's all there is, that one future that will become real. It stands before you crystal clear. Everything can be seen in that one strand that has detached itself and expanded. Everything that will happen."

I stared at her for a while in silence. "But I can't see it," I said at last. "That's what it's all about. It seems that only you are privileged to see it."

For the first time since we'd started talking, the smile disappeared from her face.

"You don't believe me, do you."

"It might be easier to believe you if I could understand why someone who has access to the future decided to kill herself. We're still coming up against this issue."

She bowed her head, resting her chin on her chest. Her hair was like a veil covering her face. From behind this came only the gentle sound of slow breathing. When she spoke, her voice was muffled and somehow far away.

"What do you think: what decides which of the strands will start to glow? What decides which of the countless possible futures will become real?"

"You've got me there," was my reply after pondering briefly. "Chance, perhaps?"

She sighed deeply. "Chance, yes. That's what I thought at first. Then the ability I have acquired would still be bearable."

As she didn't continue, I asked cautiously, "If it isn't chance, then what is it?"

She raised her head again. Her hair fell back and parted, revealing the middle of her face. She reminded me of a picture I'd seen on a billboard somewhere. "Not what, but who," she said, more softly than before.

I looked at her several moments, eyes blinking. "Someone chooses which future will become real? Who could that be?"

"Isn't it obvious?"

I made a rueful face. "I'm afraid not. At least not to me."

A shadow of a smile returned to her lips, as though wanting to forgive me for my lack of insight. "I don't hold it against you. I too needed some time to see what had been standing clearly before me from the beginning to get used to it. I, of course, am the one who makes the decision, the one who singles out the strand that will prevail over all the others. I choose the future."

"You?" This time I was unable to suppress the disbelief in my voice. "How?"

"It's actually very simple. That's what led me astray. As I look at the beam of all possible futures, my eyes under my eyelids are not quite focused. So the strands are slightly blurred. But as soon as I fix my eyes on one, it starts to detach itself. In the beginning I mistook the cause for the effect. I thought that my eyes focused on the strand that had singled itself out for some other reason, without my having anything to do with it. But things, unfortunately, are just the opposite."

We spent about half a minute in silence. Katarina clearly felt that she had now explained everything quite satisfactorily, and at first I didn't know how to continue the conversation. Suddenly, all my experience working with patients like this no longer seemed to help. I finally found my cue in her last sentence.

"Why 'unfortunately'? Isn't being able to choose the future far more advantageous than only being able to see it? Now I understand even less why you wanted to take your own life."

Katarina's face took on the expression of a teacher with a dull-witted pupil in front of her. "What's so advantageous about it?"

"Why, you could choose a future without suffering, misery, hardship. There must be some like that among those countless strands you mentioned."

She shook her head slowly. "Utopia? Heaven on earth? Don't be naive. There is no such future. Not a single strand is without suffering, misery and hardship."

"I wasn't thinking idealistically. What I had in mind was a future in which there was very little of that. One in which most people lived happily."

"But there would still be unhappy people."

"That's inevitable, you said so yourself."

There was something reproachful, accusing in her eyes. "Would you consent to be the one to choose who should be sacrificed on the altar of the happy majority?"

She'd caught me by surprise again. My hand was already reaching mechanically for the top of my head, but I stopped it at the last moment. Scratching my head suddenly seemed out of place. "That's a very difficult question."

"Yes, it is. And just think about what a heavy burden it is for someone who, without the slightest desire, has to decide which future will become real, knowing in the process that this will inevitably bring suffering, misery and hardship to someone. No human shoulders can hold up under that. I doubt that even God's shoulders are strong enough. There is only one force capable of dealing with this chilling responsibility: the blind and impassive force of chance. I have to give back to chance what belongs to it, as soon as possible, since it has reached me by some mistake. I hope that now you understand why I have no choice."

"But suicide is certainly not the only solution."

"It isn't? What else do you suggest?" Her voice was filled with sarcasm.

"You told me that this... beam of strands of the future... only appears when you close your eyes in a waking state, isn't that right?"

"That's right."

"Well, then, don't close your eyes except when you go to bed."

She shook her head back and forth. The ends of her long blond hair swayed as though blown by a gentle breeze. "If only things were that simple. You give me way too much credit. Do you really think that any human being could resist such temptation, could have such self-control? In any case, I tried that already. It was the frustration I felt after it failed that led me to that clumsy suicide attempt."

"Which didn't succeed, thank heavens."

"It didn't. Because it was so clumsy. There was anger and despair behind what I did, and they are poor allies if you want to do a job properly. It was only later, after I'd calmed down a bit in here, that I started to think things over coolly and collectedly." Her smile widened. "As you can see, there's an upside to being put in a straitjacket."

"That's not the only one. In a straitjacket, which is indeed rather uncomfortable, you are effectively prevented from doing something reckless. No one has managed to kill themselves in one yet."

"Then I will be the first one to succeed." I detected a hint of pride in her voice.

"How?"

"You'll soon find out. Things are underway and nothing can stop them."

"Are you quite sure about that?"

"Of course I'm sure. Don't forget the powers at my disposal. That's what finally crossed my mind, sitting here on the floor, as the anger from my failed attempt slowly dissolved. Why embark on something uncertain and questionable when everything can be carried out without fail?"

"You mean... ?" I made a vague circular motion with my hand.

"Yes. All I had to do was choose the future in the beam where my suicide attempt succeeds. It didn't turn out to be quite that easy, however. I picked through the strands for three full days, searching for the right one. And I finally found it."

"Which means that we are already in that future?"

"We are. And it shows you how choosing what will happen is connected to inflicting pain on others. In this time strand, Dr. Sonja falls down the stairs. I feel really bad about it. She was kind to me and full of understanding. Please ask her to forgive me. Try to explain that it simply couldn't be avoided. Your efforts will be in vain, however. You won't be able to convince her, because you will never believe it yourself. Not even after you find me dead here tomorrow."

My eyes slowly looked around the inside of the padded room. I have never liked these mournful, white isolation cells, but now it seemed the most appropriate sanctuary for this girl who clearly was still in the throes of sinister thoughts. Restrained by the straitjacket, this was the only place where she was completely safe from her own self. I've had patients with suicidal tendencies from time to time, but they were all much more typical, ordinary cases. Never before had I heard such an intricate and unbelievable story. And she told it so convincingly. Working with her would be difficult, but also challenging. I would try to talk my colleague Sonja into letting me handle Katarina's case or at least work together with her on it when she returned from sick leave.

"Of course I won't find you dead, Katarina," I said, in a voice I hoped was the epitome of conviction and self-confidence. "You will be alive and well when I come to visit you tomorrow. How could it be otherwise? We will continue our conversation then. It is extremely interesting."

She did not reply to this. A shadow of sorrow and compassion seemed to pass over her face, like a teacher who finally realizes that all her efforts have been in vain, that her pupil is too dull-witted to understand the simple things she has explained to him.

I took the file and got up from the floor. I gave two sharp knocks on the doorframe and the attendant's face appeared in the peephole almost the same moment. Evidently he had been standing in front of the door. I nodded my head. When the heavy door opened, I turned toward the girl.

"Goodbye, Katarina," I said cheerfully.

"Farewell, doctor," she replied, no less cheerfully, as if we were two friends parting after a pleasant chat, smiling warmly at one another.

I didn't find her dead the next day. She hadn't meant it literally. When I arrived at the sanatorium her body had already been taken away. The initial doubts about the cause of death had been solved as well. When her breakfast had been taken in at eight o'clock they'd found her curled up on the floor in the position in which she always slept, with her back to the door. One look at her face was enough for them to realize that she was no longer alive—Katarina's pretty face was completely deformed, grotesquely bloated and distended. Whatever had caused this ugly death mask was no longer in isolation cell number seven, so it was not clear what had actually happened until the forensics report arrived.

Katarina was allergic to wasp venom. Sometime early in the morning, between six and half past six, an insect, which could only have flown in through the opening up by the ceiling, had stung her on the left cheek. She died some twenty minutes later. Certainly before seven. There was only one problem. The girl must have been wakened by the sting. Why hadn't she called for help, since she was perfectly aware of the risk she ran? She'd had enough time, but had done nothing.

I was the one they expected to answer this question. I did so in my first and last report on Katarina. The reason she hadn't reacted was most likely because the sting enabled the execution of her previously failed attempt. It was a very unusual suicide that had taken advantage of an unbelievable tangle of circumstances. Indeed, what are the chances that a wasp will find its way through such a small opening right into a room with an individual who is allergic to its sting? Completely infinitesimal, one would say. But it happened just the same. Perhaps such holes should be closed up for this reason. In any case, they are almost useless. And you never know when and how such an inconceivable incident might occur again.

I said nothing about the motives that had led the girl to raise her hand against herself on two occasions. What could I have said, anyway? I'd had only one chance to talk with her, and that was certainly not enough to come to any reliable conclusion. Perhaps my colleague Sonja would be able to shed more light on the case, since she'd spent more time with Katarina. When I had finished my report, I got in my car and headed toward her house. I wanted to tell her the tragic news in person. And give her the message that had been sent the day before.

geese in the mist

3

The ski lift stopped about one third of the way up the slope. That was the last straw. If I'd been alone on the two-seater I would have cursed out loud. Instead I swore to myself, which wasn't the same. Only a coarse profanity would have let me vent my feelings. Some days nothing goes right. When that happens the best thing is to stay in bed, but we never know what awaits us, of course, so we dash headlong into the future like geese in the mist.

First there hadn't been any hot water in the bathroom. Irate, I'd called hotel reception only to learn that something was wrong with the boilers. I was kindly advised not to worry. The repairmen were at work and there should be hot water early in the afternoon. This information comforted me as my teeth chattered under the icy shower. As if this wasn't enough, the plastic shower cap slipped off my head for a moment, partially wetting my hair, so I had to wash it, although I hate doing it in cold water.

Then came the incident in the dining room. I shared the table with a family of three who had apparently never learned civilized behavior. During every meal the father would return from the buffet table with a great deal more food than he could possibly eat. He always left more than half of it on his plate. And he was proud of the fact. Plus, he chomped on his food with his mouth half-open. In addition, he always had a newspaper spread out in front of him.

The mother was excessively talkative and inquisitive. She didn't hesitate to adopt an intimate, chummy manner toward me even though I maintained a persistently reserved, formal demeanor and was several years older. She inundated me with questions, one of which was repeated every time we met. She was determined to find out why I had gone skiing alone, even though I'd made it perfectly clear more than once that I did not intend to disclose that information to her. The fact that I wasn't with anyone aroused her suspicions.

The son, somewhere around five or five-and-a-half, was a restless soul. He fidgeted in his chair, made a mess of the table, dropped his silverware on the floor, talked too loudly. His father paid not the slightest attention to this and his mother would mildly reproach him only when he had really gone too far. As soon as he started to play with the large bottle of ketchup, I had a feeling something unpleasant would happen. As I hesitated, wondering whether to ask the boy's mother to take the bottle away from him, he pointed it at me and squeezed.

I don't think I was his intentional target, but nonetheless a thick stream suddenly gushed across the table and hit me in the middle of my chest. A large red spot blossomed on my white sweater, as though I'd been wounded. I jumped off my chair, not knowing what to do in the initial confusion. The little boy started to giggle and his mother finally did what she should have done before it was too late. Taking the bottle and putting it on the table, she said to her son, in a not-so-angry voice, that in future he should be careful of the direction in which he pointed the ketchup.

The father's reaction pushed me over the edge. As though doing something perfectly natural and expected, he got up, put down his newspaper, took a linen napkin, and without a word began wiping it over my breasts, removing the ketchup! I looked at him in disbelief for several moments, as the desire to slap him rose sharply inside me. Nonetheless I held back, mumbled something angrily and left the dining room, feeling a large number of inquisitive eyes on me.

As I tried to wash the spot out of my sweater as best I could with cold water, the weather changed. This happens very quickly in the mountains. When I entered the bathroom, the window had been filled with completely blue sky. Less than ten minutes later, the sky had turned into a gray rectangle with no depth.

This was all I needed. Of the five days I had been there, two had been spent in the hotel because bad weather had put skiing out of the question. I needed to head for the slopes as soon as possible if I didn't want this day to be ruined too.

As I hastily tightened my bootstraps in the ski room, I tore the nail on my right index finger. I bit my lower lip, as I always do when overcome by anger. If there's anything I can't stand, it's a torn nail, but I would have wasted a good fifteen minutes if I'd taken off my boots, gone back to the room where I had some nail scissors, and then come back down to put my boots on again. I put on my mittens, hoping they would at least lessen the damage, but knew that the torn nail would keep bothering me until I took care of it. Everything was conspiring against me.

On emerging from the ski room, I found myself in a cloud. I could only see a few yards in front of me. From time to time the ghostly figures of other skiers materialized out of the dense wall of gray. I slowly made my way toward the foot of the ski lift, afraid that it might not be working. When the cloud cover is complete or a storm is blowing, they shut down the lifts. Fortunately there was no wind, and if I had any luck at all, only the area around the hotel would be veiled in mist, while the slopes at a higher altitude remained bathed in sunlight. At least, that's what I hoped.

I let out a noisy sigh of relief when I saw the moving line of skiers waiting to get onto the ski lift. Finally, something good was happening in a day filled with nothing but bad luck! My satisfaction, however, did not last long. It was lessened by the person who sat next to me on the two-seater. The man had been behind me in the line and I hadn't had any reason to turn around, so I didn't see him until he appeared next to me on the lift. He didn't do anything to annoy me; his appearance alone was enough.

I have always been irritated by non-skiers who take skiers' places on the lifts instead of hiking through the mountains, which would be much healthier and more beneficial for them. In addition, the man was by no means suited to this place. Even if one disregarded his age—he must have been in his sixties—he had dressed in clothes more suitable for an evening on the town than trekking about the mountains in this weather: hat, bow tie, white scarf, long fur-trimmed coat, thin leather gloves, umbrella, fancy shoes. He would have a great time when he got out at the top. I smiled with a certain suggestion of malice and, as much as the cramped two-seater allowed, turned my back on him.

We had already come out of the cloud when the ski lift shuddered to a halt. I knew the reason immediately: the power had failed yet again. This had happened every day since my arrival. The hotel reception had a ready explanation for this inconvenience, too. The worn-out grid was being renovated. Starting next season there would be no power outages. I felt like gnashing my teeth. Next season! A lot of good that would do me here and now. Here I was, hanging helplessly a good fifty yards up in the air, in the company of a man who was probably the last person I wanted next to me, without the slightest idea of how long it would take for the power to come back on.

As though reading my thoughts, the man suddenly addressed me: "Don't worry. The lift will start working in seven and a half minutes."

I have never been one to talk to strangers, particularly when I don't find them likeable and am in an awful mood, as I was at that moment. My first thought was not to reply, but then I would appear immature and impolite. I would have been happier if he hadn't said a word, if we had spent that time in silence as we hung there, caught between heaven and earth, but now I had no choice. Social considerations, however, did not require me to be excessively polite.

"Really, seven and a half? You must be clairvoyant!" I made no effort whatsoever to hide the mockery in my voice. I turned my head briefly toward him, with an ironic smile, then turned away from him again.

"I'm not," was his simple reply.

The conversation might have ended there. If I had not said another word, no one could have reproached me for being rude. But the rage that had been gathering inside me all morning wouldn't let me stop.

"Then how do you know exactly what's going to happen?" This time I turned my head toward him for a bit longer and was thus able to get a better look at his face. He looked exactly like my idea of a retired civil servant: plump cheeks, thick well-groomed mustache that didn't go over his lip line, small watery eyes. His aftershave lotion had a pungent, piercing odor. I don't know where I got the impression, but I was convinced that he was either a widower or unmarried.

"It's not hard, if you know the cause. Then it's easy to predict the effect."

"So you know what caused the power failure, even though you were sitting here on the ski lift when it happened? Congratulations!" My voice was still sarcastic.

"It's my job, ma'am, to know," replied the man simply, as though this explained everything. My derision clearly had not gotten through to him. "The ski lift was stopped by the failure of a tiny part in the power sub-station. It's smaller than a matchbox. Such a tiny cause, and such a huge effect." He indicated the long line of seats in front of us filled with irate, impatient skiers.

"Isn't that utterly interesting!" I knew I had gone too far, but his equanimity was driving me mad.

"Yes," he replied, taking my words literally. "The future is most often shaped by small things, very rarely by incidents of large proportions. Take, for example, the fact that we had no hot water in the hotel this morning."

"You're staying at the hotel too? I haven't seen you."

"That's because I'm inconspicuous. People don't usually take any notice of me, which is useful." He stopped briefly, hesitating. It seemed as though he'd been about to add something to his last sentence, but then decided to leave it unsaid. "The hot water heater broke down because of simple carelessness on the part of the man who maintains it. He let sleep get the upper hand and didn't do what he should have. And just see how many people had to take cold showers this morning as a result."

I was suddenly filled with unease. It seemed as though I could see the frosted glass on the shower door in my suite gradually turning transparent, making me visible to inquisitive eyes.

"Yes," I said, for the first time in a normal voice, "very unpleasant. In addition my shower cap slipped off by accident and my hair got wet." I instinctively touched the ends of my hair under my woolen hat. It was unnecessary, of course, because I had dried my hair with the hair dryer before going out.

"Accident, yes," repeated the stranger. "A vague concept used as a good excuse for ignorance. There are no accidents, ma'am, only our lack of information."

I was angered by the superior tone in his voice. I have always felt an aversion toward men who show off their alleged intelligence.

"But how could I know in advance that my shower cap would slip off? You can't predict something like that!"

He looked at me several moments without speaking. "Perhaps," he said at last. "But even you could have foreseen what happened to you in the dining room."

The anger that had just subsided flared up inside me once more. Not so much for the condescending "even you," although that was part of it. I felt myself exposed to unwanted looks again, naked. "You know about that too?" I asked. He certainly must have heard the snarl behind my words.

"Of course, I was there. I eat breakfast too."

"I didn't see you."

"I told you I'm inconspicuous. My seat is in the corner, behind your back. In any case, the incident was such that no one could have missed it."

"It all happened so fast," I said, as though defending myself. "I didn't have time to get out of the way. But it wasn't the boy's fault. His parents are to blame, of course."

"You are partially, too. It must have been clear to you from the start that something bad might happen to you in such company. You should have asked them to move you to another table. Particularly since there was no special reason for them to put you there in the first place. The waiter did it indiscriminately, just as he did with the other guests. He could have given you another seat in the same way. Had he done that, your sweater wouldn't have a spot of ketchup on it now."

"But how can the waiter be blamed? He certainly could not have guessed what would happen."

"I didn't say he was to blame, just that his arbitrary decision was the cause that led to adverse effects. Fortunately, they are harmless in this instance."

I shot him a piercing glance. "Have you ever tried to remove a ketchup stain from wool?"

"No, I haven't. I don't suppose it is easy. What I wanted to say is that even the permanent loss of a sweater would be nothing dramatic. It is simply an unpleasant matter, basically nothing more serious than, let's say, tearing your fingernail."

I stared at him suspiciously, inadvertently wrapping my right index finger in the other fingers in my mitten. I didn't have a chance to say anything, however, because the ski lift started to move at that very instant. The seats stretching before us toward the mountaintop rose up briefly and then rushed forward like a team suddenly whipped by a coachman. The man pushed up his left coat sleeve a bit, looked at his watch and nodded in satisfaction. "Exactly seven and a half minutes, just like I told you."

He might have expected me to show a bit of admiration, but I didn't. I was haunted by completely different thoughts. "You say accidents don't exist?" I asked in a low voice.

"That's right, they don't," he agreed, also speaking more softly than before.

"So that means that you're not here by accident either. Who are you, anyway? What do you want from me?"

He didn't answer right away. We covered half the distance between two ski lift towers in tense silence, staring each other in the eye. I tightly grasped the handles of the ski poles in my lap, slightly raising the pointed ends toward the other side of the seat. We were almost at the halfway station in the middle of the slope. All I had to do was raise the safety bar and quickly slide off my seat. I doubted he could have prevented me from doing it.

"Rest assured," he said at last. "You are in no danger from me. I don't want anything from you. I am only an observer."

"Observer?" I repeated questioningly, not knowing what else to say.

"Yes. I am here to see what you do. Nothing else."

"What do you mean, what I do? Isn't it obvious? I'm going to ski down the mountain. What else could I do?"

"There are many ski runs down the mountain."

"So? What difference does it make?"

"If it made no difference, I wouldn't be here now."

"I don't understand you. Do you mean to say that I will be in danger, if I take one run and not another?"

"You? No. You are completely out of danger."

"Then who isn't? Please stop playing guessing games with me. I'm not at all in the mood."

Silence followed once again. The halfway station was quite close. I raised the safety bar, ready to push off down the rise that reached up to the bottom of the seat. I expected him to say or do something, but he just looked at me wordlessly. We stayed like that without moving as we passed by the halfway station. The ski lift employee standing in front of the hut made of roughly hewn wood looked at us briefly, without interest. When he was behind our backs, I lowered the bar.

"I'm not playing guessing games with you," he said with a slight tone of relief in his voice, as though pleased I hadn't gotten off the lift. "The fact is I am allowed to tell you very little. You must make the decision all by yourself. Any involvement on my part would create enormous difficulties."

"But what decision? You've still got me confused."

"Which run you choose to ski down the mountain."

"Why is that important? This run or that. They all lead down, don't they?"

"That's right. But what happens afterward is not the same. Each run has its own continuation in the future. It is the start of a chain of events and each has a very different outcome. Fortunately, most of these outcomes are pretty innocuous, but some are not. Sometimes, not often, ordinary causes, such as which run you decide to take down the mountain, can result in truly catastrophic effects. You've heard the story of the butterfly harmlessly fluttering its wings and ultimately causing a hurricane on the other side of the world? Of course the butterfly is not to blame, but should one stand idly by and do nothing to interrupt the chain of events that leads to misfortune?"

At first I didn't know what to reply. The confusion that overcame me had muddled my thoughts. I stared dully at his round face, ruddy from the cold. His cheeks were dappled with a network of winding capillaries, like those of a drunkard. He looked back at me with steady eyes in which I thought I could detect impatience and expectation.

And then, as though the internal mist clouding my mind weren't enough, one started on the outside, too. It all happened in a split second, as usual. One moment we were traveling up through the brilliant blue mountain morning sky, and the very next we were in the middle of a dense, gray, almost palpable mass. With my attention distracted, I hadn't noticed the direction from which the cloud had come. Probably from below, otherwise I would have seen it before then. Everything suddenly became unreal around us. We seemed to be floating in nothingness. If it weren't for the empty seats that appeared at regular intervals going in the opposite direction, only visible when they were quite close to us, we would not have felt that we were moving at all.

"What do you do to prevent a disaster? Kill the butterfly, I suppose, before it flutters its wings? Remove the cause before it happens?" My voice was trembling slightly, although I tried to say this as calmly as possible.

"That would be the simplest thing, yes. Unfortunately, that cannot be done. You have to let the cause happen, and only then react."

I let out a deep sigh, then inhaled a breath of air. It was filled with tiny, prickly drops that would be used as the raw material for some future snow. "But how is it possible to tell which butterfly will cause the disaster? There are countless numbers of them."

"It's possible," replied the man tersely. I waited several moments, hoping he would add something more, but he remained silent.

"What is it about me that singles me out from the other skiers? Why is it important which ski run I in particular take? What if you are mistaken, what if I am not at all the right person?"

"We are not mistaken." Once again his self-confident brevity didn't tell me a thing.

"And that's all the explanation you have to offer?" My voice was tinged with anger again. "You appear out of nowhere, tell me a twisted, fantastic story and expect me to believe you."

"It isn't necessary for you to believe me." It seemed that nothing could shake the man's composure. "I am aware of the fact that my words must seem confusing and unconvincing. But I can't tell you anything further without disturbing an order that must remain untouched. I have actually told you too much already. The best thing would be for you to act as though we had never met, as though this conversation never took place. We will soon reach the top of the mountain. Get off the ski lift and simply take one of the runs down the slope. Don't even think about which one. Do it spontaneously, like you always do."

"Simply forget this ride up the ski lift? As though I came up to the top all alone?" It was impossible for him not to hear the mixed hurt and disbelief in my voice.

"That would be best. In any case, you will never see me again. Nor will you find any trace of me at the hotel; it will be as if I never set foot on this mountain."

I chewed my lower lip and nodded. That instant the cloud became drenched with brightness and started to thin. Soon we were above it, in perfectly clear air. The bright blue sky and sparkling white snow forced me to squint, and I lowered the sunglasses that had been pushed up onto my hat. We were almost at the top. The two skiers on the seat in front of us were just getting off.

I raised the safety bar slowly. I did not take my shielded eyes off the man on the seat next to me. I knew that he would not say anything else to me, and I had no desire to say anything to him, either. Maybe he was right, after all. Why not pretend that this meeting had never taken place? Isn't oblivion the best protection against the ugly occurrences that take place in life?

I slipped off the ski lift seat, made a short turn to the right, and stopped a bit to the side of the path that skiers were taking down the slope. I stuck my poles into the snow in front of me and leaned on them. The seat I had just been on moved forward to a covered area where a huge horizontal wheel slowly turned. The seat made a semicircle around the wheel and then headed in the opposite direction, downhill.

The man did not let me out of his sight. First he turned around in his seat to keep me in his field of vision, and then when he realized that wouldn't be enough he got up and kneeled on the seat, without taking care to lower the safety bar. The ski lift employee in front of the hut at the top shouted something at him in warning, but the stranger paid no attention. He stayed in the same position, holding onto the back of the seat as he rushed inexorably toward the edge of the cloud. He was too far away for me to make out the expression on his face, but it was easy to imagine.

I let the doughy gray matter swallow him up completely, then waited a few more moments. When it was certain there was no way he could see me, I did what was expected of me. Quite spontaneously, without thinking, I headed down one of the runs. Like I always do. It was highly irresponsible with regard to the future, I know, but that responsibility had been forced upon me. I hadn't accepted it voluntarily. In addition, even if such a future were devoid of disaster, I would only be a puppet, my strings pulled by someone else's invisible hands. And if there is one thing I simply cannot tolerate, it is someone manipulating my life. Regardless of the pretext.

Several moments later, when I too plunged into the gray lake, I thought with a smile that we actually don't understand geese. Dashing headlong into the mist doesn't have to be the least bit unpleasant.

line on the palm

4

I carefully examined the client at my door. This is extremely important in my work. A person's outward appearance says a lot about his future. Or rather, about what he would like to hear about his future. People don't go to a clairvoyant to be told bad news and then have to pay for it. They don't need someone like me for that. What they expect from me is help, as they would from a doctor or clergyman. And I provide this help. The basic motto in my line of work is: the customer must leave my parlor satisfied. After that, things take their own course.

Actually, if I were to predict that something bad was going to happen, I'm certain almost no one would believe me. This seems to be part of human nature. If you tell people something that suits them, they all accept it eagerly, regardless of how implausible or even impossible it might appear. Sometimes it seems the more incredible the favorable prophecy, the easier it is for them to accept. They don't quibble. And of course, if you tell them something that doesn't suit them, they immediately become doubtful and suspicious. They launch into a debate on reliability, and then on the meaning of divination, endeavoring to show it's all pure quackery that only the gullible would swallow. If that's true, then why on earth did they come to see me?

The customer's age made him unusual from the start. Mostly middle-aged people visit me. Younger people are not overly bothered by the future because they think they have it in abundance. They have all the time in the world before them. Older folks know they don't have any future, so it doesn't interest them very much. Between the age of forty and fifty, however, people start to settle their accounts. And the realization of their own mortality is always part and parcel of this. Although almost no one would be willing to admit it, what brings a great many people to my parlor is the newly aroused fear of death. What they want most of all from me is a guarantee that judgment day is still a long way off. And of course I provide this guarantee—at a very moderate price, even though they would be willing to pay much more. One mustn't profit from the misfortunes of others.

The young man was no more than twenty-five years old. I don't remember a younger person ever coming into my parlor. His height was emphasized by a long, olive-drab raincoat with broad lapels. A lightweight white scarf was thrown casually around his neck, its ends reaching almost to his waist. He had a long face with regular features, more masculine than handsome. His thick black hair was combed straight back from his high forehead. He wore small, round, wire-rimmed glasses. Shortsightedness at his age probably resulted from years of intensive reading. His umbrella was in its sheath, hooked over his left arm.

He was wearing thin, black leather gloves that made his hands invisible. That's the first thing I examine in any customer. If you are skillful at noticing things, which I must be in this job, hands can reveal a vast amount of useful information about a visitor. Shoes as well. The young man's shoes were clean and polished in spite of the bad weather—even overly clean. This indicated a finicky individual, inclined to nit-picking, someone who has difficulty changing an entrenched opinion. The way he'd tied his laces indicated someone who liked orderliness, regularity, symmetry. It was unlikely he could see nuances. Only extremes: either-or. This was not exactly a good sign. It was much easier to work with less orderly, more easy-going visitors. The ones I liked the best were actually those who paid no attention at all to their appearance.

He hovered at the door to my parlor, examining it with the same curiosity that I turned on him. This was clearly the first time he'd come to a place like this. His eyes skimmed through the semi-dark room, absorbing the details. I was certain that he was taking it all in, that nothing escaped his attention. His lips suddenly pursed into a grimace of disapproval, even disgust, when he saw the little glass boxes on the small shelf to the left of my worktable. They contained several specimens of what were erroneously believed to be traditional trappings of the fortune-telling trade: the wing of a bat, tail of a rat, eye of an owl, tooth of a wild boar, skin of a snake, claw of a hawk...

I don't like these things either. That's why the shelf is positioned outside my field of vision when I sit at my worktable, where I spend most of my time. But these things have their purpose. They impress the customers. The great majority of my visitors come with a completely stereotyped notion of what a fortune-teller's parlor looks like, so I don't dare let them down. Everything here is set up and modeled after what you'd find in a popular film.

The finishing touch is a small cauldron of water—electric, but a fire seems to be underneath it—with wispy steam rising in a column, colored pink by the beam of a hidden red light. From time to time a strong, seemingly exotic fragrance emanates from the steam, although what I put in the water to get it is something quite ordinary. Whenever possible I try to avoid using that fragrance additive because after a while it gives me a headache and even makes me nauseous.

When I felt I had given the new customer enough time to inspect the parlor, I bowed briefly and said, "Good evening, sir. Please sit down." My hand motioned toward the chair on the other side of the table.

"Good evening," replied the young man, staying by the

door. If I'd heard his voice over the telephone, I would have said he was at least ten years older.

Periodically I have a visitor who, after entering the parlor, seems instantly to regret having done so, and would like to leave without delay. Two or three have almost run out of the room, horrified, after spending less than a minute inside. Those who make it through that first minute usually stay. I know from experience how best to act toward reluctant customers who can't seem to detach themselves from the door. I strike up a conversation about something innocuous, neutral. So they can relax. Afterward everything is a lot easier.

"It's not raining," I said half-questioningly, nodding toward his umbrella in its sheath.

"No, it's not," he said in confirmation. "Mist has set in, although the weathermen forecast rain. That's why I brought it."

"Weathermen," I repeated with a proper dose of derision. "Don't count on weathermen when it comes to forecasting the future. They don't know a thing about it. They pretend what they're doing is some sort of science, but all they really know how to do is make an educated guess. And most often it turns out to be wrong."

"But it's not like that here, is it?" His voice took on a tinge of irony.

"Of course not," I replied, feigning offense. "Would you come here if you thought I had no more skill than a weatherman?"

"The fact that I came doesn't prove a thing. Maybe I shouldn't have. Just like I was wrong when I listened to the weather forecast and brought an umbrella."

"Perhaps. But there's no way to know until you've tried it. Since you've already given the weatherman a chance to show what he can do, it wouldn't be fair not to give me the same chance." I inserted a brief, tactical pause. "In any case, just to show you how much I believe in my abilities, here's what I propose. Although the usual practice here is to pay in advance, you don't have to. I will only take my fee at the end of the séance and only if you are satisfied." This always works. People feel safe if they don't have to pay in advance for what might be bad news. Since there never is any, of course, they willingly pay in the end. It's not unusual for them to add a big tip, so when they leave there is mutual satisfaction.

He looked at me without speaking for a few moments. "But you can't know in advance whether I'll be satisfied. What if you predict something I don't like?"

"I'm prepared to take that risk," I said self-confidently. "Please, sit down." As he continued to stand indecisively by the door, I added with a smile, "Don't worry, nothing will happen to you." This was another tried and tested method with my male visitors. The easiest way to break them is to touch on their vanity. What, me afraid of an ordinary little old fortune-teller? With the ladies the same results are achieved using a calculated touch of flattery.

He finally left the door and came up to the table. He stood in front of me for a moment, confused, not knowing what to do with his umbrella, and then he hooked the handle on the back of the chair and sat down. I could have suggested he leave the umbrella and raincoat on the coat rack by the door—the parlor was heated, of course—but I didn't because I was suddenly convinced that he would refuse. He seemed like someone who only feels safe in the armor he has put on, sword in hand. Without them he would be naked and vulnerable, like a knight in a bedroom.

I didn't get down to business right away. In keeping with well-established protocol, I first looked him piercingly in the eyes for a good fifteen seconds, not saying a word. Few visitors are able to withstand this meticulous inspection. The others lower their eyes quickly and start to fidget. This assures that authority has been achieved. The conversation that follows is similar to that between a doctor and his patient or between a priest and a member of the flock. But the young man didn't flinch; his dark brown eyes calmly returned my gaze through the thick lenses of his glasses. In the end I was the first to withdraw, aware of the fact that a difficult séance awaited me. It couldn't be helped, though. Unfortunately, I was not in a position to choose my customers. Fortunately, such visitors are quite uncommon.

"So, you'd like to know what the future holds for you?"

"That's why people come here, isn't it?"

"Yes, by and large. Which of the procedures would you like

to use? All the classic methods are available." I started to show him the paraphernalia in front of me. "Gazing into a crystal ball, reading several types of cards or the leaves from a cup of tea you have drunk. There is also throwing beans, pieces of wood or bones. And astrology, of course. For a supplementary payment the future can be foretold through the entrails of a freshly slaughtered animal, although this requires special preparations. Particularly if the customer chooses a larger species. Such as an ox."

At this point I always smile broadly in order to show the horrified visitor that I am only joking. Usually I get a smile in return, often accompanied by a sigh of relief, but the young man's face retained its serious expression.

"If none of these techniques suits you," I hurried to add, "even though they have proved successful for thousands of years, there are also new methods. We could use a computer, for example." I turned my head toward the monitor on the corner of my large worktable. The fact that it was under a plastic cover with a thick layer of dust on top indicated the interest my customers had in modern forms of predicting the future. "I have an excellent, professional divination program. Imported."

"I'd like you to read my palm. If you do that."

"Of course I read palms," I replied in a tone that was intended to express, more than the words, just how amazed I was at such a question. "I didn't mention it because no one has asked for it in quite some time. It seems like palm reading has gone out of fashion. You may have been unaware, but fashions change in fortune-telling just like in everything else. Although, with palm reading, this is somewhat peculiar, since the palm is part of your body and can thus be considered the most direct, reliable indicator of your fate. I think you have made a good choice."

The young man, who until then had kept his hands in his lap, hidden from my view, slowly raised his right hand and laid it palm up on the green felt that covered the middle of the table, illuminated by a narrow beam of bright light.

I waited several moments, but since he wasn't about to do anything, I said, "It might be helpful if you took off your glove."

The gloomy seriousness of his face softened for the first time. "Sorry," he said, with an expression of discomfiture. He wasn't quick about it, however. He took off the glove with slow movements, almost with reluctance. He suddenly reminded me of a striptease artist starting her act. When he was finished, he briefly held his hand clenched in a fist before opening it up—apparently against his better judgment.

I didn't look at his palm right away, as some shoddy diviner would do. If you want your customer to take you seriously in this work, you have to respect formality. And formality here required that I first take a bit of cotton, put some alcohol on it and briskly rub the surface of his palm with it. Although the reason for this should have been obvious, many visitors were bewildered and asked for an explanation. I gave them one, trying to make it sound as professional as possible, sprinkled with

Latin words.

After having thoroughly cleaned his palm, I took a large magnifying glass with a handle and frame of imitation ivory, wiped it with a gray linen cloth, and finally looked at his palm.

Even under the magnifying glass the young man's life-line appeared quite short. I had seen other lines that suddenly stopped or branched somewhere around halfway to the base of the hand, but never one like this. It barely reached one-third of the way. If there really was something to this, my young visitor should already have met his maker. Luckily for him, this was just plain superstition. Luckily for me, that was quite widespread. Neither of us had any reason to complain.

I raised my head and looked him in the eyes. It was only then that I realized this had not been tactically wise. I should have continued calmly examining his palm as though there was nothing special on it. This way, he received confirmation that something was wrong. I quickly returned my eyes to his palm, but it was too late.

"I'm going to die soon." He said it in a soft, flat voice, as though stating an incontrovertible fact.

"Excuse me?" I asked with exaggerated surprise, not taking my eyes off what was under the magnifying glass.

"I don't have much longer to live."

"Why do you think that?"

"My lifeline."

"What about it?"

"See how short it is."

"I see. And so?"

"That means my time is almost up."

I laid the magnifying glass on the table and looked at my customer again. The calculated harshness in my eyes expressed legitimate indignation.

"My dear young man, if you know how to interpret the lines on your palm, why waste your time and money with me?"

I don't resort to this sentence very often because the occasions to use it, thank heavens, have been rather rare, but whenever I've said it the effect has always been as expected. This time, however, the effect was missing. Judging by my visitor's face, the rebuke had made no impression at all. I would have to act even angrier.

"It's simply amazing how some people fail to realize that palm reading is a very serious and responsible craft, and not something that just anyone can do. Skill is only acquired after thorough training and long experience, and natural talent is absolutely necessary. In this respect, it is not very different from medical diagnostics. Would you interfere in a diagnostician's work?"

The young man did not reply immediately. Something seemed to be weighing on his mind. When he finally answered, he disregarded my rhetorical question. "Do you think I might live a long life?"

I sighed deeply and picked up the magnifying glass again.

This seemed to have done the trick. I bent over his palm and started to examine it once more. I did it slowly and meticulously, taking lots of time. With ordinary customers I stated my verdict relatively fast in order to create the impression that everything was clearly and easily readable. With such smart alecks, however, I had to do the opposite. They are only convinced if the prediction is made after exhaustive and lengthy examination.

"You will live a relatively long life," I said at last. "I guarantee at least 84.5 years, although there is a chance that you might live to 90."

Not a single customer, regardless of how distrustful they are in the beginning, has failed to light up when they hear they have decades of life before them. Sometimes there are even touching moments, with tears and sincere confessions about the dark forebodings and fears that have brought them to my parlor. Some of those who have been relieved of a particularly heavy burden have even fallen into my arms. In those moments, as I pat them on the back, I feel proud of my line of work. Gone is the guilty conscience that haunts me from time to time. What people get from me, at a modest price, is measured not by how true or honest it is, but by how useful.

There was not even a flicker of a smile on the young man's face. "Guarantee?"

Now he really had gone too far. I had yet to encounter such ingratitude. "Of course I guarantee!" I almost shouted. "I can give it to you in writing if you want!"

My agitation didn't sway him. "But your guarantee can be easily invalidated," he said in a steady voice.

"Is that so?" His composure only fed the flames of my anger. "And please, won't you tell me just how?"

"Easily. I could kill myself."

I thought I hadn't heard correctly. "You could do what?"

"Kill myself," he repeated, as though stating the obvious.

I stared at his wooden face. I had underestimated this customer. He wasn't just one of the ordinary skeptics who come in periodically. I know how to deal with them. This was quite a different case. I'd never had a visitor who mentioned suicide, nor had I heard of any such customer visiting my colleagues. The young man certainly wasn't serious, but I still had to be careful. If anything were to happen, they might close my shop.

"Of course you can't kill yourself," I said in a tone that restored my previous composure. "Even if you wanted to. What is clearly written on your palm would prevent you. You will die an old man, whether you like it or not. Indeed, I see no reason why that shouldn't please you."

"But I can," replied the young man. With a rapid movement he pulled his right hand from the lighted circle on the felt and stuck it between the lapels of his raincoat. A moment later he pulled it out, holding a gun. I don't understand a thing about weapons, but this one seemed serious and threatening enough in spite of its small size. He held it in front of him, the barrel turned between the two of us.

I knew I had to say something if I wanted to retain control of the situation, but try as I feverishly might, nothing coherent crossed my mind. I just stared dully at the shiny, chromium-plated metal in the visitor's hand, feeling a lump form in my throat. I had never been that close to a firearm before.

"What's stopping me?" said the young man, breaking the silence. "It's quite a simple matter." He cocked the gun with his thumb and put it next to his right temple. "All I have to do is pull the trigger."

"Wait!" finally burst out of me. I jumped halfway out of my chair.

There must have been something funny about that because the visitor's lips curved into a gentle smile. He didn't put the gun down, but his finger relaxed on the trigger.

"Why?"

"You'd kill yourself just to prove that my prophecy isn't true?" The fact that my voice was shaking certainly didn't help, but there was nothing to be done. I slowly sank back into my chair.

He hesitated a long moment and then lowered the gun into his lap, out of my sight. An audible click meant the gun was no longer cocked. A loud sigh of relief escaped me.

"I would kill myself to foil predestination. That's the only way I have to beat it. I've thought about it for a long while. When you're marked like I am, you don't have time for much else." He raised his hand without the gun, turned his palm toward me briefly, then put it back in his lap.

"But I told you... "

"I know what you told me," he said, cutting in. "But it's all the same, don't you see? Instead of one predetermination you offered me another. And one that is considerably longer. Isn't it enough that I've suffered for almost two decades because of what's written on my palm? Should this agony now continue into old age? You can't imagine how heavy a burden it is. I simply wouldn't be able to bear it that long. It's utterly impossible to live if you know when you will die."

Silence fell on us like a heavy shroud. Even if I hadn't been experienced at interpreting my visitors' expressions, it was easy to read what was in the young man's eyes: a suicide's firm resolve to follow through on his intention.

"But if you didn't want to find out when you will die, why did you come to my parlor?"

"I didn't come to your parlor to find out when I will die. I know that already. I came here because this is the most suitable place to kill myself. The temple of predestination. It is only here that my act will have true meaning."

"This is no temple of predestination," I said in a muffled voice, like a criminal admitting guilt when faced with incriminating evidence.

"What else is a fortune-teller's parlor?" asked the young man, knitting his brow.

"A temple of false hopes. Those who decide to visit me

don't do it for the sake of truth. Somewhere deep inside them, everyone is aware of that. What brings them here is the suddenly aroused awareness of their own mortality. The same that has started to haunt you much too early. Indeed, I don't offer them the eternity they would be promised if they went to church. What I sell doesn't last quite that long, and so has less value. But there are those who would buy longevity."

"False longevity."

"False, of course. What else could it be? There is no true prediction of the future for the very reason that there is no predetermination. You are ready to raise your hand against yourself in order to beat an opponent that doesn't even exist."

"But my lifeline... " He raised his hand again, this time with the gun in it.

"Your lifeline doesn't say a thing. And neither does mine. Or anyone else's. It's all pure superstition. What is written in your palm has nothing to do with how long you will live. Right now that depends entirely upon you. You can pull that trigger and follow through on an enormous misconception. Or you can forget the whole thing and embark on an uncertain future, enjoying the very uncertainty it holds."

As I spoke these words, I tried anxiously to guess what his reaction would be. My worst fear was that he would pay absolutely no attention, finding my words false or not convincing enough, and would simply end things the way he had clearly intended when he came in my parlor. Another possibility, certainly less ominous although still very troublesome, would be to embark with me on a metaphysical discussion about predestination, waving his weapon under my nose all the while as his trump card. Curiously enough, I was least repulsed by what in any other circumstances would have appeared the most horrendous threat: that he would sue me for openly admitting that I consciously deceived my customers, even with noble intentions. That would certainly have closed down my parlor.

The young man sat there for a long time in silence, staring at me fixedly. Or maybe the time seemed long to me. Time can pass very slowly when you are waiting for something stressful. When he finally spoke, I was speechless with surprise for several moments.

"How much do I owe you?" he asked.

"You don't owe me anything, of course."

"No, please. I have to pay." He stood up, still holding the gun. His other hand picked up the glove on the table, then his umbrella from the back of the chair.

There was no sense arguing. How can you refuse money from a man brandishing a gun in front of you? I stated the lowest price that I keep only for special customers. This one certainly belonged in that category, so my generosity was well founded.

My visitor was suddenly in a predicament. Since both hands were full, he couldn't reach his wallet. Finally, he tucked the gun back inside his raincoat, fumbled around inside a bit, then took out his wallet. The banknote he handed me was considerably larger than the sum I'd asked for.

"I'm afraid I don't have change," I said in an apologetic voice. "If you could wait a minute, I'll go change it. Just around the corner. I'll be right back."

"There's no need to give anything back. Keep the change."

I didn't have a chance to protest because the young man made a brisk about-face and headed for the door. I thought he would leave without a word, but he stopped at the door, turned and said, "Good night."

My answering "good night" echoed in the empty parlor.

I stayed in my chair, staring blankly at the large banknote, turning it over and over between my fingers. Like a mantra, this monotonous, rustling sound helped me pull myself together. Life has taught me one thing: always look on the bright side, whenever possible, even in the most difficult situations. Although the visit that just ended had certainly been unusual and in many ways unpleasant, there had been no adverse consequences.

The most important thing, of course, was that I had prevented the young man from committing suicide, something that would have been quite detrimental to us both. He would clearly have been in a far worse situation, but I would have had my share of trouble too. If only he'd found some other reason to raise a hand against himself than just outwitting predestination! As if predestination existed; or rather, if it existed, as if it were at all possible to outwit it. A bonus was the fee. It would have taken at least five customers for me to earn what this visitor had left me so gallantly. And the days when that many people enter my parlor can be counted on one hand.

Finally, the incident I had just gone through started me thinking about putting in special security measures. We live in uncertain times, and additional precautions certainly couldn't hurt. Besides, I am visited by strangers who are all, without exception, burdened with troubles. Carefree, satisfied people don't go to see a clairvoyant. I'd been lucky this time, but I certainly didn't want some future customer to pull a gun on me. Maybe I should put an inconspicuous metal detector by the entrance, similar to those at airports. Provided it wasn't too expensive, of course.

I was roused from my thoughts by a sharp ringing. Usually my customers barely touch the doorbell, dreading what awaits them inside, but whoever was at my door now clearly wasn't the slightest bit afraid. Judging by the insistent ringing, for some reason he must have been in a great hurry to find out his future.

"Coming, coming," I shouted, getting up from my chair.

As I shuffled toward the door on limbs that had gone numb from sitting so long, it suddenly occurred to me that it might be the young man. He'd changed his mind and decided to do what he'd originally intended after all. Panic-stricken at this possibility, I stood there without moving, my hand on the doorknob, not knowing what to do. But the ringing simply wouldn't stop, so I finally opened the door a crack and peered into the dense mist that filled the evening.

The face I saw was not the young man's. In front of the door was a rather short, middle-aged man with a bushy beard, wearing a winter coat. I had never seen him before. His appearance, however, did not bring relief. He seemed upset, as though he'd just been through an ordeal.

"Excuse me, ma'am," he said in a trembling voice, unconsciously taking off his hat, exposing his balding head. "Yours is the only light that's on. Would you mind... letting me use your telephone? It's urgent. There's been an... accident."

"Accident?" I repeated.

"Yes, here—quite close," he said, motioning vaguely toward the left. "A young man was crossing the street. I didn't see him in the mist... I was driving slowly, of course. Suddenly he popped out in front of me—out of nowhere. I didn't have time to hit the brakes. It all happened so suddenly... "

"Is he injured?" I asked, although it was unnecessary. As an experienced clairvoyant, I had to know the answer.

"I'm afraid he's dead, ma'am. He's lying there—on the pavement... covered with blood." He raised the bloody, white scarf in his hand. "I tried to stop the bleeding with this—he died in my arms. I have to call the police... "

The police soon arrived and made an inspection of the scene. There was no investigation since there was no need. It was a clear-cut case. Inattentive pedestrians periodically meet their end like that in the mist. There was nothing the driver could have done.

No one asked me anything. Why should they, anyway? I wasn't a witness to the tragic event. I didn't offer to make a statement either. What for? Why would the police be interested in what some old fortune-teller thinks about a routine traffic accident?

alarm clock on the night table

5

Miss Margarita's eyes popped wide open. She realized instantly that something was wrong. Lying there in bed, staring at the ceiling, she tried to figure out what had given her this impression. Had it come from her dream? But she couldn't remember dreaming anything. That was odd because she always had dreams, and always remembered them. Then she realized what was wrong. She was surrounded by silence. Turning her head toward the night table on her left, she looked blearily at the round old alarm clock with its phosphorescent hands and two dome-shaped bells.

It had been sitting there for more than half a century. Its ticking had only bothered her briefly in the beginning. She'd soon become used to it and now could not fall asleep without its steady metal throbbing. Once a year, when she took it to the watchmaker to be cleaned and oiled, she would lie awake in bed for a long time, sometimes all night. Miss Margarita used the clock only to fall asleep, not to wake up. During all these years she had never once set the alarm. There was no need for that; she was one of those rare individuals with a reliable internal clock, able to wake up at a precisely set time. Not a minute early or late.

The night before she had set her internal clock for 7:30. There was no way she could have failed to do this, for it was an invariable part of her preparations for sleep. After coming out of the bathroom, she would bring a glass of water from the kitchen covered with a saucer, although she rarely woke up at night and even then was hardly ever thirsty. Then she would read in bed for about a quarter of an hour, always from the same book, a slim collection of love poems that had been with her as long as the clock. She had learned them all by heart ages ago, but read them nonetheless. Finally, after turning out the light, she would simply wish to wake up at the usual time. That was enough. All that was left was to close her eyes and surrender to the lulling ticking of the clock.

The clock hands were now standing in a position that could not be correct: 12:07. Even though Miss Margarita's eyesight had faded, she could still make out the long, black hands against the white surface with its Roman numerals. All the same, she reached for her glasses, which had been placed next to the water on the night table where she could find them easily in the dark. After putting them on she saw more clearly, but what she saw hadn't changed. The clock had evidently stopped right after midnight. This was the first time it had stopped working completely.

She would take it to the watchmaker's right after breakfast. This would disrupt her day somewhat, but what choice did she have? She led an orderly life consisting of a well-established round of obligations. She didn't like to deviate from it because postponing or neglecting her duties filled her with unease, and once that crept into her soul it was hard to get rid of. But this was an emergency. The alarm clock certainly had precedence. The thought of the clock standing broken on the night table, with her doing nothing to fix it, would upset her even more. In any case, the sooner she gave it to him, the greater were the chances that the watchmaker would fix it that very day, so perhaps she would not be without it the next night.

She had a quick breakfast. She knew her sensitive stomach might complain, but she couldn't eat any more slowly. Fortunately, the meal was light, as it was every morning. She crumbled one and a half slices of day-old bread into a cup half-filled with warm milk. The milk contained one teaspoon of chicory and half a teaspoon of sugar. Indeed, the sugar was always a bit more than half a teaspoon, but she considered it to be half nonetheless, scrupulously following her doctor's orders. If she hadn't been in such a hurry, she would have waited for the bits of bread to absorb the milk completely and become soggy.

But now she didn't have the patience, so she had to chew them instead of letting them slide down her throat.

It didn't take her long to get dressed either. She had two dresses for outings during the summer. She wore the less formal one to do the shopping and take her afternoon walk in the park, while she kept the other one for rare special occasions such as this. She stood in front of the mirror for a moment, deep in thought, and then decided to put on a brooch. She didn't like jewelry and decorations, but she decided that without any accessory she would look somehow incomplete. The greatest amount of time was spent putting on her little black hat with its lace veil. Unfortunately, this could not be helped. Before, when her hair was still luxuriant, she had put her hat in place with ease, but her hair had thinned with the years, making it harder and harder. Finally, she dabbed on some perfume from a small bottle with the label half peeling off. Then, fearing that was not enough, she dabbed on a bit more.

Outside she was greeted by a bright summer morning. The air was preternaturally transparent, as though rain had just washed all the dust out of it, but there was no trace of recent precipitation. Everything was dry, announcing yet another hot day. Smiling, she headed for the watchmaker's shop, a twenty-minute walk away. She had gone about one third of the way when she was struck once again by the feeling that something was wrong.

She stopped and stared intently ahead. Then she turned

her head around slowly and looked behind her. She might have stayed in that position longer, but the ossified vertebrae in her neck soon started to complain. There had been no need for such exertions, however. Just one glance was enough to confirm that not a living soul was anywhere to be seen. She was completely alone in the middle of an empty street. And not only that. She suddenly became aware of something that the intoxicatingly bright morning had obscured. She had not seen a single person since leaving the house.

Strange. She went to the grocery store every day at this time and always met someone along the way. Even in the worst weather. That was her entire social life. Since she had no friends to visit or to come and visit her, the only chance she had of talking to anybody was when she ran across acquaintances from the neighborhood each morning. There were only strangers in the distant park and her walks there were silent. Her morning conversations in the street were not particularly profound: health complaints, passing on local news, exchanging thoughts about the weather, occasionally reminiscing about some bygone event. But she always felt satisfied and fulfilled afterward, and the solitude of the rest of the day was easier to bear.

Why wasn't there anyone about? She mulled it over briefly but could find no explanation. She finally shrugged her shoulders. She certainly couldn't stand there waiting for someone to appear. She had to hasten on her way. Maybe the watchmaker would be able to tell her what was going on. There must be a simple answer, but she just couldn't find it. He would probably think her a senile or even dim-witted old woman when she asked. The best thing, actually, would be not to mention it. Was it all that important whether there were people in the street or not? This way was even better, as though the beauty of the day belonged to her alone.

When she was almost there, she realized there was something missing in this beauty. The row of chestnut trees along the street was usually full of birds, particularly in the morning and evening, tirelessly chattering, competing with the rustling leaves in the treetops. Now only the breeze could be heard up there. Where had they all gone? There was no time to dwell on this matter, however, because another, more important one prevailed. What if the watchmaker wasn't there? What if he hadn't come to work and had gone somewhere like everyone else? That would be really hard to take. Who would repair her clock?

There was a sharp jangling of bells above the entrance when Miss Margarita opened the door. She glanced toward the counter facing her and let out a sigh of relief when she saw the hunched figure of the watchmaker, a tube-shaped magnifying glass placed on the socket of his eye. He was engrossed in a repair job. He removed the magnifying glass, raised his head, squinted toward the entrance, smiled and stood up.

"Hello, Miss Margarita."

"Hello," she replied cheerfully and headed toward the

counter.

As she slowly made her way, she noticed a change on the side walls of the little shop. She remembered quite well from earlier visits that there had been two identical grandfather clocks in mahogany cases. They rang out the hour in deep, harmonious tones and seemed very formal, like soldiers in dress uniform guarding the entrance to a castle. She'd envied the watchmaker. She would have been very happy to have such a clock in her parlor, but her income did not allow this. She had not even dared ask how much they cost.

Now both walls were completely covered with alarm clocks. They came in all types, shapes, sizes and colors, from elegant to ugly, from ornate to plain. Their bells were what differed most. She seemed to be at a dolls' show of metal hats worn by inappropriately stocky models. Those with two or three hats were particularly grotesque, which probably meant they had two or three heads. Then she noticed something that hadn't immediately caught her eye. The clocks weren't working. If they had, a deafening cascade of ticking would have gushed from both sides of the shop. No one would have been able to stand such noise for very long. The watchmaker did not wind the clocks after he placed them on the wall.

When she reached the counter, Miss Margarita took the alarm clock wrapped in white flannel out of her brown shoulder bag.

"It's broken," she said dejectedly.

The watchmaker took the bundle and started to unwrap it. He was a small, thin man with long side-whiskers and a high forehead. He was wearing a dark three-piece suit of classic cut, with subtle gray stripes. The only accessory was the silver chain of a pocket watch hanging from the buttonhole on his vest, leading to a small pocket on the left-hand side. It was hard to determine his age. The best guess would be late middle age. Miss Margarita had concluded long ago that he was one of those people practically untouched by age. The long intervals between the times she saw him seemed to have had absolutely no effect on him.

"Is it slow again, like last time?"

"No, it's not. It's stopped."

"Completely?" he asked in surprise.

"Yes, completely. Last night, right after midnight. You can see for yourself. I haven't touched a thing." Miss Margarita paused, waiting for the clock to emerge finally from the cloth, and then added, "I hope it's nothing serious."

The watchmaker in silence made a cursory examination of the clock lying on the unwrapped cloth on the counter. She tried to figure out the diagnosis by the expression on his face, but it remained completely blank.

"I'll have to open it up," he said at last. "Please take a seat; it might take some time." He indicated two armchairs with a small table between them to the left of the entrance.

Miss Margarita nodded and went to sit down. She would

have been just as obedient if she'd been asked to leave the operating room and wait in the waiting room while they operated on someone very close to her. She would have cast the same worried glance toward the place where the vitally important business was taking place. But she couldn't see very much. The watchmaker was hunched over, practically under the counter, working on a lower bench located in the back. All that appeared was the upper half of his head, with the watchmaker's magnifying glass once again in place, almost touching the green shade of the lamp brightly illuminating the workbench.

The silence of the multitude of clocks hanging over her, behind and in front, started to weigh her down. Although she detested noise, she now felt it would be easier to stand if they were working. It would be confirmation that time was flowing. This way, it seemed as though time had stopped and the operation on her clock could last an eternity. Nothing moved around her; the inside of the shop, together with herself and the watchmaker, seemed to belong to a pictured moment, frozen forever.

The picture nonetheless soon came to life. The watchmaker slowly took the magnifying glass off his left eye, got up, took the clock from the workbench and placed it on the flannel cloth on the counter. He then took it in both hands, went around the counter, approached Miss Margarita, and sat in the other armchair.

"I'm afraid there's nothing to be done," he said in the voice of a doctor whose patient has just had a sheet pulled over his head. "Here, see for yourself."

He put the cloth with the clock on the little round table between them. Just then Miss Margarita noticed that the clock had not been put back together. The back cover was off, revealing a tangle of tiny gears, springs, levers, screws and pins. Her eyes remained only briefly on these mechanical entrails, for she quickly turned her head aside. She was overcome by nausea, as though looking at an open human body in an anatomy class. The watchmaker did not notice this movement, and had already started to explain.

"These two gears here are broken. They're worn out. Unfortunately, they are highly important. You might say they are the heart of the clock. And nothing can work without a heart, isn't that so? If this were a newer model it would be easy to replace them, but no one makes spare parts anymore for such old models. The manufacturers are better off selling you a new one." He sighed and turned to look at the wall covered with silent clocks. "Just like your clock, all of these could have kept time and woken people up, if only there had been parts for them."

"But I don't need a clock to keep time and wake me up." She'd thought she would never reveal her secret to the watchmaker, but now she had no choice.

The watchmaker looked at her, puzzled. "What else could an alarm clock be used for?"

She did not reply at once. She felt ill at ease, as though having to answer a doctor's questions regarding something deeply intimate. But how can you expect the doctor to help if you hide something from him?

"To fall asleep," she answered at last, softly and reluctantly. "I can't fall asleep without its ticking."

"Then maybe you should think about buying a new one? It could serve that purpose, while also carrying out all its basic functions. There's no harm in having them, even if you don't use them. I will be happy to buy your old alarm clock, so a new one won't cost very much. As you can see, I collect them." This time he gestured toward the multitude of clocks.

"No!" said Miss Margarita, almost screaming. "I won't sell it!" And then, ashamed of such a violent outburst, she hurried to add, "It's a memento, you know, a very dear one, from..."

The sentence was left unfinished, but the watchmaker nodded nonetheless. "I understand. Please let me take another look at it. Maybe something can be done if all you want is for it to tick."

He put his hands under the cloth again and took the clock behind the counter. This time the wait seemed different to Miss Margarita. Her previous apprehension was replaced by impatience. She felt naked before the watchmaker and wanted this to end as soon as possible. Whatever the result of his attempts, she would no longer have any reason to go to this shop. If the clock ticked, all the better. If it didn't, she would certainly not buy a new one. Where would she keep it? Next to the old one on the night table? That would be nothing less than sacrilege.

She would simply have to get used to falling asleep without any help. It would certainly be difficult, at least in the beginning, but what other choice was there?

From the smile on the watchmaker's face as he returned carrying the alarm clock, this time with the back cover in place, she understood she had nothing to fear.

"You were in luck," he said after sitting in the armchair. "From now on your clock will tick if you wind it regularly, although it will always show the same time." He started to wrap it in the flannel cloth. "That part of the mechanism is still in working order. It shouldn't wear out for quite some time. Here you are." He handed her the large bundle across the table.

"Thank you," she said, taking the wrapped clock. As she put it in her bag she could hear the soft ticking, muffled by thick layers of cloth. "How much do I owe you?"

"Goodness, nothing. It was such a small thing."

"Please, I insist... "

"Miss Margarita, I doubt whether you will be needing my services anymore. Consider this a small farewell present. You have been a loyal customer for many years. This is the least I can do to repay your fidelity."

She had never liked people to give her services free of charge. If she were to insist on paying now, however, the watchmaker might take offense and this was certainly something she wanted to avoid. Particularly if this truly was, as he felt, their last meeting.

"Thank you once again. I still remain in your debt." She stood up and he did the same. They stood in silence for several moments, and then she said briefly, "Goodbye."

The watchmaker bowed. "Farewell, Miss Margarita."

She turned and headed for the door. This was the first time she'd left this shop sad and not pleased. Just a few minutes earlier she'd wanted never to come here again, and now she hoped he was wrong. The alarm clock was old, it might break down again. That would give her the chance to bring it back for repairs. Suddenly it became important for this not to be her last visit to the watchmaker. She didn't like the hint of finality that went with it.

When she went out in the street, her first thought was that her eyesight had blurred for some reason, just like in winter when her glasses suddenly fogged up as she entered a heated room out of the cold. But it wasn't winter now, it was the middle of summer, plus she wasn't wearing glasses. Indeed, she saw better with them on, but she felt they didn't look good on her, so she preferred to strain her eyes a bit instead. Now even the strongest glasses would not have helped her see through the curtain of mist that had descended while she'd been inside. This was the exact opposite of the air's previously ethereal quality. The world that had seemed perfectly clear before had now become completely opaque.

She leaned her back against the shop door to obtain firm support. Wrapped in grayness that made it impossible to see even the pavement on which she was standing, she seemed to be floating in midair. She stayed there without moving for a time, not knowing what to do. She thought about going back inside, but then she would be faced with having to explain and would only become hopelessly muddled. No, that was out of the question.

What else could she do? She certainly couldn't stand there for very long. Then a simple solution appeared that did, however, require considerable ingenuity and courage. She would head home. Just like that. Where else would she find refuge on such an unusual day but in her house? It wouldn't be easy to get there since she couldn't even see her fingers in front of her eyes, but luckily all she had to do was move straight ahead. There were no turns. She would go slowly and carefully, using the row of chestnuts as her guide. The trees were placed at regular intervals so once she counted the steps between two neighboring trees, she would know exactly when to expect the next one.

It took great strength of will to leave the shop entrance and walk into the mist. Somewhere from the edge of oblivion flashed a memory from her far-off childhood when she was learning how to swim. Then she had been forced to overcome tremendous internal resistance to leave the shelter of the shore and venture out into deep water. The buoy she'd headed for was only several yards away but to her the distance had seemed immeasurably far. She'd hugged it feverishly when she finally reached it. Now she was tempted to grab the chestnut tree in the same way, its outline only starting to emerge when she was already quite close to it.

She went slowly down the street, holding one arm out in front like a blind person holding a white stick. Her eyes were wide open, although useless. All they saw was the fluffy dough in which she was immersed. She soon felt dizzy from staring into the unchanging whiteness. She thought of continuing with her eyes closed, but couldn't find the courage to close them and bowed her head instead. After the seventeenth step, when she almost crashed into the second chestnut, the relief she felt rivaled that of a castaway thrown fortuitously onto land by a storm.

She continued with somewhat greater confidence, concentrating on counting her steps. This feeble encouragement soon evaporated when she realized that she would not be able to tell when she'd reached home. The tree growing in front of her house had nothing unusual about it, and she didn't know how many chestnut trees there were between her home and the watchmaker's shop. She had never counted them, of course. Why would she? Who would ever have thought it might come in handy? She stopped, bewildered, and then continued her slow steps. She would ponder that problem along the way. A solution was bound to turn up. Right now it was important to advance in the right direction.

Her hampered eyesight sharpened her hearing. She was between the sixth and seventh chestnut when she heard soft voices coming from somewhere in the mist. How strange people were, she thought. She hadn't met anyone during the glorious weather on her way to the watchmaker's shop, and now there was someone talking outside, in this obscurity. She crossed the distance between the next three trees, but the voices were still subdued, no louder than before, as though she'd come neither closer to those who were talking nor moved any further away from them. Now, however, they seemed to be coming from the treetops, as though the birds had returned and were now chirping in the leaves with human voices.

She pricked up her ears and finally started to make out the words coming from above. They were disconnected parts of different conversations. Sometimes two people were speaking, sometimes three, and there were even more here and there. There were men's, women's and children's voices, old and young. The fragments were not long: they started in the middle of a sentence and then suddenly ended, so it was hard to grasp their meaning. Sometimes laughter would resound in different timbres: giggling, droning, chuckling, roaring. Much less frequently the conversation was serious and gloomy, and one was even filled with quiet crying.

Most of the voices sounded familiar to her. She was sure she had already heard them somewhere, but hard as she tried she could not call to mind the faces of those who were talking. This filled her with frustration. Her memory had recently started to fail her like this; she would be on the verge of grasping something, and then it would be maliciously whisked away. And then she noticed a regularity, a common characteristic of the bits of conversation from the chestnut treetops. There was a female voice in every fragment. Old, coughing, sometimes defiant. This was the moment of truth. She might still not have recognized her own voice—we don't hear our voice the same way others hear it—were it not for the defiance that was her manner of confronting the world, most often to her own detriment.

As though someone had pulled the veil from her memory, suddenly there were no more secrets. Regardless of how brief the fragment, she knew unfailingly when it was, where and to whom she was talking in these magically resurrected conversations. Her interlocutors' empty faces took on contours, features, characteristics. She saw them clearly on the occasions when they were talking to her, just as she could now remember the parts that preceded each fragment and followed it. Her life stood before her as clear as an open book intermittently underlined.

Making her way through the endlessly thick mist, hand outstretched before her, silently counting the steps between the chestnuts, she wondered whether the lines she heard spoken above were highlighted merely at random or with some purpose in mind. They were certainly not important conversations, most were just bits of small talk. It seemed to her as if someone had noted down parts of her book of life without rhyme or reason. Or else she was unable to detect any. She was just about to stop searching, when she noted a new pattern. It had to do not with the content of the fragments but with their distribution in time. Each one was further back in time than the one before it, as though the book were being leafed through back to front. The further she got from the watchmaker's shop, the deeper she retreated into the past.

Her voice became gradually younger and softer. It wasn't hard for her to imagine the increasingly younger face that went along with it. Her wrinkles smoothed out, the loose skin hanging sadly under her chin disappeared, the spots on her cheeks vanished and so did the yellow bags under her eyes. The many aches that had started to plague her in old age also faded away. She'd lived a healthy and tranquil middle age that from this vantage point had been possibly the happiest period of her life. She'd been alone, indeed, but that was something to which she had already become quite accustomed.

Most of those she now heard herself briefly talking to were no longer among the living. She had considerably outlived them all. She ascribed this primarily to her orderly lifestyle. The others had been their own worst enemies, not paying enough attention to their health. She knew that the most dissolute among them secretly made fun of her self-discipline and moderation, mockingly calling her ascetic, but she had been the one in a position to laugh last. She had never done this, however. She had been defiant and stubborn, yes indeed, but not malicious. The loss of each one had been hard for her. Tears came to her eyes even now as she heard their long-silent voices return once again above her.

The closer she got to her younger years, going home through the mist, the greater became her apprehension. It had taken a lot of time and effort to block out the incident from that time that had shaped all the rest of her life. Perhaps everything would have been different had she been able to wipe it completely from her memory, but that, of course, had been impossible. Although suppressed, it was still with her, reemerging from oblivion, often at the most inopportune moments. She had no way of knowing how these audible fragments from her past would treat the incident, but she felt certain they could not ignore it.

Her anxieties came true, but not as she had feared. Judging by the number of chestnut trees she'd counted, she must have already been close to home when the noise in the treetops suddenly ceased. She stopped in bewilderment and listened hard. Now she longed for the surreal voices that had frightened her at first. Without them she felt hopelessly abandoned in the hollow silence of the mist. Then she heard a soft sound somewhere behind her. It was repeated at regular intervals, becoming stronger, as though the source were moving closer to her. She didn't recognize it until it was almost upon her. Someone was walking down the street, heading in her direction.

Judging by the spryness of the steps, it must have been a younger man who did not seem the least bothered by the mist. Miss Margarita stood stock-still, fearing there might be a collision. He didn't know she was standing there and might easily run right into her. She had to find some way to let him know she was in front of him. She cleared her throat, but at the same moment realized this was unnecessary.

Like the beam of a reflector sliding through the darkness, dispelling it, a clear oval bubble was making its way through the mist, moving down the street. When it came close to her she had a good look inside. The young man was tall and slender. His face had firm, regular features that were handsome in their accentuated masculinity. The rather long, slanted scar above his left eyebrow did not spoil this harmony; on the contrary, it even seemed to add to it in some strange way. The officer's dress uniform fit him perfectly. He was wearing high, polished black leather boots, soft white gloves and a service cap pulled down low on his forehead, almost completely hiding his short hair. In his left hand were two small packages wrapped in brightly colored paper and tied with red ribbons. One was flat, the other square.

Miss Margarita's breath failed her. She opened her mouth and made every effort to breathe deeply, but she suddenly seemed to be in an airless space. In addition, she was unable to move. Her heart began to pound frantically. The stiffness did not last long, however. She snapped out of it when the grayness surrounded her once again, after the oval had passed. She took out after it almost at a run. The doctor had strictly forbidden such efforts, but that made no difference to her now. Once she had caught up with the oval she continued at a somewhat slower pace, panting as she kept to its rear edge.

It was the safest way to reach home. The young man would take her there without fail. The mist was no longer an obstacle. The path stretched before her as clearly as that which would inevitably come to pass. He soon turned off the pavement onto a narrow stone walkway leading across the grass to the front door. When he took off his cap and rang the bell, Miss Margarita was standing hesitantly about halfway up the walk. She knew who would open the door to him, but it seemed somehow inappropriate, almost unnatural, to look at that person. In addition, she was still very angry with her. After all these years she still could not forgive her for what she had done.

The door opened, but the young man's broad back almost completely blocked the entrance to the house. For just a moment, before the door closed, she caught sight of the hem of a light yellow dress fluttering in the draft. She still had it, but kept it out of sight so as not to awaken painful memories. Miss Margarita remained on the walk, not knowing what to do. She was still out of breath, but not just from having moved so fast. The fact that she could change nothing in that far-off past that was taking place before her once again weighed more heavily on her than any physical exertion. Since it served no purpose inside the house, the oval bubble stayed outside, resembling a tiny island in a vast downy ocean, waiting for the young man whose visit would be of short duration.

The closed door did not prevent her from seeing what was happening inside. She accepted the two little packages with delight. She had always loved presents. She untied the ribbon on the flat package first. Smiling broadly, she went up on her tiptoes, closed her eyes briefly and lightly touched the young man's lips with hers in thanks. It was just a hint, a suggestion of a kiss, but their intimacy had not yet gone any further. The deluxe edition of the poems looked magnificent. She'd wanted it so much! And how much she had wanted to receive it from him!

She couldn't imagine what was in the other package. Her impatience got the better of her, as usual, so she pulled the ribbon and tore the bright wrapping paper. She quickly raised the lid of the square, purple box and looked inside inquisitively. Her smile instantly disappeared. Her face flared up as though she'd just been slapped. She shot him a look in which insult, reproach and the accusation of betrayal vied for precedence. She felt her eyes fill with tears. She stood there for several moments, staring at him without a word, and then did what the sharp voice of her defiant, proud nature commanded. She roughly put everything she was holding into his hands—wrapping paper, ribbon, book, box and the item inside it—turned and quickly walked out of the parlor. She almost slammed the bedroom door behind her.

She leaned against the inside of the door to prevent him from coming after her. How could he have done such a thing! After everything that had happened, the alarm clock was not only an insult but an injury. Two days earlier, while they were walking along the quay, why had she mentioned her ability to wake up whenever she wanted, without any outside help? She'd exposed herself to someone who was unworthy of it. He'd just laughed, almost as though mocking her. He'd said he didn't believe her, that no one could do something like that. And then, as though this were not enough, he'd added in a playful voice that he might believe her if he had the chance to see for himself.

She hadn't immediately understood the full meaning of his words because she was unaccustomed to such allusions. When it finally dawned on her that seeing her ability for himself meant waking up in the same bed, she turned on her heel in anger and quickly walked away from him along the quay. How could he think something like that? Who did he think she was? Why, they weren't even engaged yet! And even if they were, it would still be highly improper. He ran after her and when he reached her started to apologize, but she turned him a completely deaf ear. It was not until they were near her house that she spoke to him, her voice cold and official. She told him that he had greatly offended her and she never wanted to see him again. Never. She didn't give him a chance to say anything in reply. She had turned her back on him once again and gone into the house.

Her anger lasted all through the evening, but softened the next morning. That was also part of her nature. Remorse was the flip side of her defiance. By noon she had already shifted the blame to herself for being so hard on him. Maybe he hadn't thought anything bad; it had just been a clumsy joke; probably he'd been unaware that such a joke might hurt her. In the evening the pangs of guilt from such serious questions were almost physically painful. What if he took literally what she'd said to him at their parting? How else could "never" be understood except as "never?" She could have gone looking for him and explained that "never" was not quite as final as it might appear, but that, of course, was out of the question. Her pride would not let her regret go quite that far.

The next morning he'd come to the front door in the dress uniform he'd been wearing when she first set eyes on him four and a half months before and fell immediately in love. A flood of joy streamed through her. She could barely stop herself from falling into his arms right then and there, on the doorstep. Only a few minutes later, however, had come the terrible slap with the alarm clock. Leaning against the bedroom door, she did not even try to hold back her sobs. It made no difference to her that he would certainly hear her in the parlor. Nothing made any difference anymore. This time "never" would be absolute and irrevocable. The only thing she wanted was for him to leave. To disappear from her parlor. And her life.

And he had left. The parlor and her life. First he'd put the opened presents he'd brought on the table. They belonged to her and she could do what she wanted with them. He certainly couldn't take them where he would soon be heading. He hadn't had the chance to tell her the main reason for his visit. He thought briefly about knocking on the bedroom door and giving her the order that had reached his house late last night. In less than three hours he would board a train that would take him straight to the front. But he hadn't knocked. He already knew her quite well. She would never open the door for him. He turned slowly around the room as though wanting to fix it in his memory. Then he put his cap back on and went out.

The oval bubble was waiting in readiness to clear his path through the mist that he didn't see. Just as he didn't see the tiny, stooped old woman he almost brushed against. If he had been able to hear through the chasm of time that separated them, her sobs would seem strangely familiar to him. But he couldn't hear. She, however, heard the sound of his departing footsteps long after the opaque grayness closed behind him. She stayed on the walk, her eyes turned toward the invisible street, until silence reigned around her once again. Then she walked the remaining bit of cobbled path to the front door of her house. The mist had once more enclosed her on all sides, but she no longer had to walk with her hand outstretched.

She went straight to the bedroom. That was where she kept a chest full of mementos. There were faded photographs, yellowed letters, items greatly damaged by the ravages of time: a past significant to her alone. Among these old things was a wilted piece of paper. She took it and slowly started to read the four lines typed on it, although just like the book of poems, she had learned them by heart long ago. This text was not the least bit lyrical, although whoever had drawn it up had taken pains to give it a lofty ring. Telegrams sent by the army to families of the dead always sound somehow wrong.

She had received it only three days after leaving him in the parlor and locking herself in this room. She was not related to him, but her name had nonetheless been on the list of those to be informed in case of his death. The officer who had brought the news added awkwardly that there had been no funeral. The general slaughter at the front offered little opportunity for that, and it was rare for very much of the deceased to be left to bury. After the war, of course, a great charnel house would be made for all the fallen heroes, and she would be invited to the conse-cration. She had never been invited, and she wouldn't have gone if she had. Her connection to it certainly was not the same as that of the others.

She put the telegram back in place and closed the chest. She stood next to it for several minutes, not knowing what else to do. What time of day was it? The vast mist outside made it impos-sible to tell by looking out of the window. This reminded her of the clock in her bag. It, unfortunately, could not help her find out the time because it no longer worked. Too bad. She had no other clock in the house. She would have to buy a conventional one. She didn't care very much about knowing the exact time, but one could not live without a clock, after all. She would keep it somewhere in the parlor or kitchen.

She took the alarm clock out of her bag and put it on the night table, then sat on the bed. The clock's hands were fixed on the time it had stopped, but it ticked steadily as though still measuring something. She stared at it blankly. She stayed like that until she felt the repetitive sound starting to have an effect on her. It was certainly not yet time for bed, but this unusual day had completely exhausted her. Maybe she would stretch out a bit, just to have a little rest. She didn't even have to get undressed. She would just lie on the bedspread. She never slept during the day, let alone fully dressed, but what difference did it make? There was no one to see her. In any case, she was not accountable to anyone for her behavior.

She closed her eyes. Before she sank into the deep darkness and silence, two thoughts briefly crossed her mind. She was somehow convinced that she wouldn't have any dreams. That was good. She would have the best rest that way. Who knew what dreams might visit her? In addition, this time there was no need to set her internal clock. She had no reason to wake up at any specific hour. No urgent work awaited her anymore.

Photograph by
Marko Todorović

A truly unique author whose work bends trusted concepts in a seductively ordinary manner, Zoran Živković has been compared to such luminaries as Italo Calvino, Franz Kafka, Jorge Luis Borges, and Stanislew Lem. His work has been broadcast on BBC radio, produced for both television and film, and published in 17 countries; by the end of 2007 two more countries will have joined that list.

He has been the recipient of the World Fantasy Award and the Miloš Crnjanski Award, as well as a two-time finalist for the prestigious Serbian NIN Award and a three-time finalist for the International Dublin Literary Award. He has been named as a Guest of Honor for EuroCon 2007.

His mosaic novel *Seven Touches of Music* appeared in the United States and Canada in 2006, and his mosaic novel *Impossible Encounters* will appear there in 2008.

The author was born in Belgrade, former Yugoslavia, in 1948. In 1973 he graduated from the University of Belgrade's Department of General Literature with a degree in literature; he received his master's degree in 1979 and his doctorate in 1982 from the same school.

He lives in Belgrade, Serbia, with his wife Mia, their twin sons Uroš and Andreja, and their four cats.

Find out more about

Steps Through the Mist

and author Zoran Živković
at www.aiopublishing.com

Reviews
Author interview
Latest author and book news
Contact Zoran

Order another copy of this book online at
www.aiopublishing.com for free shipping
and fast fulfillment of your order.

Or to order by mail, please send a request and
check or money order for $23.95 plus $3.00 for
shipping (South Carolina residents please
add applicable sales tax) to:

aio

Aio Publishing Co., LLC
P. O. Box 30788
Charleston, SC 29417
USA

Please also consider our friends to the north...
OnSpec is the Canadian magazine of the fantastic,
nominated many times over for the Hugo Award
(Best Semi-Pro Magazine). Mention this page
to them and receive a free back issue!